THE ORACLE OF
YUGGOTH

Independently published. All rights reserved. No part of this work may be reproduced, stored in a retrieval system, or transmitted in any form or by any means, electronic, mechanical, photocopying, recording or otherwise, without the prior written permission of the copyright holders. Infringement of these rights may constitute a crime against intellectual property.

© Francisco Miguel Vicens-Picatto Gual

Cover:: Francisco Miguel Vicens-Picatto Gual
Artwork: Francisco Miguel Vicens-Picatto Gual
Layout: Mabel Castillo Fernández
Translation and proof reading: Daniel Romero Rivera

ISBN: 979-82-659-5599-9

TABLE OF CONTENTS

1. The arrival 9
2. The Excavation 17
3. The Brotherhood 23
4. The Labyrinth and the Crystal 27
5. Entangled 37
6. Lost 43
7. The Descent 47
8. Ego 51
9. Eva 57
10. Flashes in the Darkness 61
11. A New Hope 67
12. The Astronaut 69

13. A long-awaited journey	73
14. Not Being	79
15. The Protocol	83
16. Desperation	87
17. Silence	91
18. The Thousand Faces of the Minotaur	95
19. The Birth	99
20. The Oracle	107
21. The Sea	115
22. The Awakening	119

Year 2283

Part of this account was extracted from the minds of Isabel Van der Velde and the other crew members of the Persephone through complex processes of regressive hypnosis. They were performed, upon their return from Pluto, in a clandestine laboratory owned by a shadowy organization known as "The Brotherhood."

Chapter 1
The arrival

The crew of the *Persephone* kept many secrets. One might speak, for example, about the true identity of Captain Pedro Diop, concealed behind that false name, or about the unspeakable sins of Aukan, a hardened mercenary who had long worked as a star pirate and hitman for The Brotherhood, the secretive organization which funded the *Persephone's* expedition to Pluto.

Yet none of those secrets, not even those kept by other crew members, were as intriguing as those kept by Isabel, a powerful priestess and worshipper of an ancient, dark deity.

Isabel's mission was to decipher an ancient mystery which her superiors suspected might lie hidden in that distant world. She was selected for such a vital task due to her long and impressive record of service to The Brotherhood.

After detaching from the orbital module, the *Persephone* and its crew headed toward the dwarf planet with a clear destination: the place where one of The Brotherhood's telescopes, a little less than an Earth year earlier, had detected a gravitational anomaly.

There, they assumed, they would find vestiges of an ancient civilization.

The mission seemed simple at first sight, but it was of utmost importance: arrive before the Confederation of Free Worlds discovered the anomaly. Every second mattered, and failure was not an option. The petty bureaucrats leading humanity's political structures could not be allowed to hinder the advancement of knowledge—knowledge that might be used to elevate the species as a whole.

As the ship crossed the void of space, each crew member prepared for what might be waiting on the mysterious planetoid. Aboard the *Persephone*, secrets, ambitions, and fears intertwined, weaving a web of intrigue that, sooner or later, would be exposed beneath the cold and dim light of distant Pluto, known to a select few as Yuggoth.

"Something's wrong," Diop announced, visibly nervous, exhaling sharply as he took manual control of the *Persephone* to perform an emergency maneuver and correct an error in the trajectory previously plotted by the ship's A.I.

He paused, took a deep breath, and added:

"I'm ordering all crew to fasten their seatbelts and remain seated while I execute this maneuver."

The crew obeyed silently, a silence that contrasted with the internal noise they all felt: the fear of death gripping them all, without exception. Only the hum of the ship's systems and the faint creaking of the hull under gravitational stress filled the air as Diop, his hands steady but his face tense, fought to keep the *Persephone* stable against the violent forces outside. Meanwhile, Harun, the onboard technician, monitored the systems from his console.

The frozen planetoid, "small" yet relentless, posed a considerable challenge. Turbulence shook the ship, and for a moment, Diop felt he was losing control. The *Persephone* seemed on the verge of crashing into the icy rocks of the remote world. But his piloting skills, honed over years of experience, allowed him to regain stability at the last moment, just as Harun was about to cry out in terror upon seeing a jagged rock formation too close to the ship.

With a nearly impossible and precise maneuver, Diop managed to land the *Persephone* at the designated location. A collective sigh of relief swept through the ship as the engines gradually powered down.

What they saw left most of the crew speechless.

From the bridge, they could see a vast architectural complex carved and polished from some kind of unclassifiable black material, gleaming in the dim light of Pluto; a light that mingled with a ghostly purple glow emanating from certain areas of the complex. Pyramids, obelisks, and strange-shaped buildings stood in an arrangement that defied any known logic. The geometry was unnatural, alien. The structures seemed to warp perception, evoking impossible forms that defied the mind and, at times, caused vertigo in the observer.

While Diop, Harun, Aukan and Kolab (the neo-psychoanalyst of the mission) stared in disbelief, Isabel Van der Velde remained unmoved. Her face showed not astonishment, but something else: a look of enthusiasm. It wasn't the face of someone surprised, but of someone who had expected exactly what they were seeing, and felt fortunate for it.

For his part, Aukan, responsible for keeping the crew safe in case they encountered any threat, knew that despite his extensive history and proven combat prowess, this was something completely different from any job he had ever done before.

In front of them, from the heart of the complex, rose a great pyramid, more imposing than any other structure, defying both space and time. From a portal near its apex, a luminous halo of an intense violet hue emerged, more intense than any other light in the complex. It seemed to pulse, alive, attracting everyone's attention.

What they saw before them was not human. That much was crystal clear to all of them. It was something dark, disturbing, imbued with an unknown purpose.

"What the hell…?" Harun gasped, visibly frightened. His voice burst across the bridge, trembling with a mix of fear and bewilderment, as he pointed toward the pyramid.

"Calm down, Harun," Aukan growled, arms crossed, his expression stern. "Screaming won't help now."

"Calm down?" Harun turned to him, eyes wide. "Are you seriously telling me to calm down when we're staring at something that clearly shouldn't exist and that, all by itself, shatters everything we thought we knew about the solar system!?"

Aukan didn't answer immediately. His gaze hardened, and his fingers reached instinctively for a weapon that was no longer where it should have been: strapped to his belt.

"Enough," Diop's deep voice, sharp and firm, cut through the tension like a blade. "This is not the time to argue."

"Argue?" Harun retorted, now addressing the Captain. "That damned light radiating from the pyramid it's not natural! Can't you feel it? There's something in that light. Something terrible. I can feel it, somehow." He looked around the bridge, seeking support in his crewmates' faces, but found only hesitant stares.

"Yes, Harun. We feel it," Isabel chimed in, striding purposefully toward the center of the bridge. Her presence was magnetic; all eyes drawned to her. "And what we feel is the call of our destiny."

"The call?" Kolab's voice was barely a whisper.

"Indeed," Isabel replied with an enigmatic smile. There was something disturbing about her, a mix of devotion and madness. "This light, this structure… They are an invitation."

"Invitation?" Aukan frowned and took a step forward. "What kind of invitation?"

"The kind that only a few have the privilege to receive," Isabel said, turning to him with a tone that carried an almost supernatural authority. "You don't understand, you're not ready for it."

"Ready?" Aukan let out a bitter laugh, thick with contempt, before snapping at them, "The only thing I'm ready for is to defend myself if this place turns hostile and to save your asses when you screw up. That's what I'm being paid for."

As they spoke, the violet glow of the pyramid seemed to pulse more intensely, as if responding to the conversation. Harun took a step back, hands trembling, certain of two things: that something was terribly wrong with this place... and that he couldn't leave until the mission was over.

Isabel smiled again, this time with visible excitement. Harun closed his eyes and muttered something inaudible, perhaps a prayer. Kolab fastened her belt, unable to look out the window as she tried in vain to calm herself.

Then, suddenly, or at least that's how Isabel and the others perceived it, they all found themselves elsewhere. They were under a dome, sitting on divans carved from a strange, porous stone, reminiscent of pumice eroded over centuries. The transition had been so abrupt that some didn't even realize they were no longer on the *Persephone's* bridge.

"Where are we?" Harun cried out, his voice trembling with panic as his eyes darted around the room, searching for something, anything, that might explain what had happened. Nothing did.

All around them, the black, mirror-like walls of the hemispherical chamber reflected their distorted faces. The space was no more than eight meters in diameter, and the only illumination came from the dizzying violet light that seemed to emanate from everywhere and nowhere all at once.

Isabel Van der Velde smiled, a serene, almost triumphant smile that contrasted sharply with the rising fear among the others.

"It seems we've somehow entered the structure," she said.

"How is that possible?" Aukan muttered, staring at her, then at the walls, then back again.

"It doesn't matter," Isabel replied reverently, rising to her feet with a fluid, graceful movement. "We're inside, and our mission is clear: to uncover the mysteries that have dwelled here for countless millennia."

Harun shook his head, breathing faster as logic struggled and failed to overcome his fear.

"This can't be right…" he murmured. "I'm just an engineer. I wasn't supposed to leave the *Persephone*. The contract didn't…"

"Shut up!" Diop barked, his voice thick with fury. The Captain stepped forward, his figure attempting to project strength, only to be swallowed by the purple glow that now filled the room. "Things have unfolded as they have, and I won't let you ruin the mission. When we return to Earth, you'll get the appropriate risk allowance. Understood?"

Harun breathed deeply and looked away, his hands still trembling.

"This room seems to have no exit," Kolab observed, trying to maintain composure as her eyes scanned every corner of the place. She searched the black walls for a crack, a door, any sign of an escape route. As the mission's neo-psychoanalyst, she was meant to evaluate the psychological impact of the expedition, but now the real challenge was keeping his head in the face of the terror inspired by both the place and the situation.

The violet light, without any clear source, seemed to saturate everything, including her thoughts. There was something oppressive in the air, as if an invisible presence was watching them from within the light itself.

"It's like we're… trapped inside something alive," Kolab whispered, not realizing she had spoken aloud until the words had already left her lips.

"We're not trapped," Isabel corrected her, moving toward one of the reflective walls.

"Captain, we need to get out of here!" Harun screamed, desperate and trembling with terror, defying Diop's earlier order.

"Silence," Isabel commanded in her firm voice, imbued with authority.

The priestess stepped forward into the center of the chamber, dimly lit by the violet glow that seemed to intensify with each word she began to recite. A deep, guttural murmur rose from her lips, evoking a strange and arcane language that echoed off the walls like a living resonance.

The others, bewildered, exchanged uneasy glances, but none dared to interrupt. They knew that some humans, like Isabel, possessed ancient knowledge and supernatural powers. With that understanding, they maintained a respectful, almost sepulchral silence, as the oppressive tension in the air seemed to envelop them like an invisible tide.

The spell reached its climax, and the confidence in Isabel's voice grew. Her final words stretched like a chant that seemed to resonate not only in space but also in their minds. With a confident gesture, she extended her hand toward one of the black walls, and everyone watched, astonished, as it passed through it as if it were made of black water.

The priestess turned to them with a calm yet commanding gaze.

"Follow me."

The fear was palpable on the faces of the rest of the crew, but the reality was inescapable: that dark surface, so solid and opaque just a moment before, was now their only way out. The alternative to following Isabel was to remain trapped in the stifling room, and none of them was willing to do that.

One by one, driven by desperation and fear, they crossed after her. Aukan was the first, tense, almost rigid, alert to any threat that might lurk on the other side. Kolab followed, murmuring something inaudible to herself, while Harun stepped forward with hesitant steps, clenching his fists in a futile attempt to contain the trembling in his hands.

As they crossed that uncertain threshold, each of them felt as if millions of purple eyes floating in the interspatial void were staring at them. It was a sensation that affected not only their senses but also their minds, as if something were examining them, laying bare their thoughts and deepest secrets.

The void completely enveloped them in the absence of everything they knew: there was no up or down, no time or space, only the eyes, those watchful orbs that seemed to peer into their souls as they floated in that ethereal state, trapped between the tangible world and something much older, more distant, and unfathomable.

Finally, their feet touched solid ground, and the void vanished like mist dispersing under a beam of light; on the other side of the portal, they found themselves in a completely different place. Isabel, standing before them, looked at them with a mix of serenity and determination.

"We are where we need to be," she said with a firm voice, full of meaning. "Now the truly important part begins."

Chapter 2
The Excavation

Year 2046, Alaska.

The wind whipped furiously across that remote and ancient frozen valley, like diamond dust, cutting into the skin of anyone not properly protected. Everything was covered by an immense layer of snow, from which only the archaeological excavation camp, set up just over two months earlier, stood out. Not even the dense pine forest surrounding it seemed capable of showing a single hint of color through the prevailing, immaculate white.

The operation, funded by a private institution whose name never appeared in official reports, was not a simple scientific exploration. Behind the appearance of a modest philanthropic initiative lay a much more ambitious and tremendously dangerous purpose.

"Dr. Raines! You need to come quickly!" The worker's voice sounded anxious and carried a hint of fear, unusual in men used to the harshness of the Arctic.

Dr. Malcolm Raines, a veteran archaeologist with a weary gaze, looked up from the map he was studying in the main tent. At his side, Dr. Evelyn Moore, his right hand, looked at him with a glint of expectation in her eyes while impatiently playing with one of the blond strands of hair that flowed over her shoulders.

"Another false alarm? Or finally something real?" she muttered, a mix of nervousness and repressed desire in her voice.

"Do you think they've finally found it?" Evelyn asked, excitedly buttoning up her coat as she followed Raines outside. Evelyn was anxious. She had always feared she would spend her life buried in irrelevant research that would make her as irrelevant as the work itself.

Raines didn't answer, but the look he gave her was filled with restrained excitement and curiosity, a look that disappeared with his figure into the relentless blizzard whipping the camp, one they had to face if they hoped to reach the location indicated by the worker.

When they arrived at the discovery site, several workers were gathered around a newly uncovered opening in the ground. It was located in an area where the team had been drilling for weeks. The snow had been cleared away, revealing what seemed to be the entrance to a tunnel carved directly into the rock. It wasn't natural. The walls were too regular, the angles too precise...

Raines and Evelyn exchanged a glance. This was exactly what they feared and, at the same time, what they had hoped for. They knew the structure had to be there, buried under millennia of ice. Evelyn exhaled with relief. Her fear of not making the breakthrough all researchers dream of had just vanished, like a sandcastle in a storm.

Some of those present thought they heard a faint sound coming from the opening. A few even claimed to have seen a reddish glow escape from that ancient prison. Others simply felt fear.

"Quick, bring the flashlights, the recording equipment, and the descent gear with oxygen tanks. We don't want to suffocate in who-knows-what ancient vapors awaits us down there! Evelyn, you're coming with me. I want to see this with my own eyes, and you have to be there. We're doing this together," ordered Raines, looking at her with overflowing enthusiasm.

Raines, a renowned archaeologist who had abandoned his lauded academic career at the Sorbonne in Paris years before, knew exactly what he would find there. Leaving everything behind hadn't been a rash decision; leading this expedition was an opportunity he couldn't pass up, and he knew it almost immediately. A private organization, shrouded in absolute secrecy, had recruited him by showing him a tablet made of an unknown blackish metal, covered in strange inscriptions, along with studies dating it as a piece of "impossible" antiquity.

But that wasn't all. According to the cave paintings found in the same cavern that housed the tablet, which were known to be much more recent than the tablet itself, these symbols belonged to an ancient race of alien beings that inhabited Earth long before humanity existed. The pictographs depicted winged, crab-like beings who had descended to Earth and, after living here for a long time, had come into contact with the first humans, who appeared long after the arrival of these cosmic entities.

Now he found himself in the heart of a desolate corner of the frozen North, convinced that this discovery would forever change the history humanity thought it knew. And it was enthusiasm that burned in his heart, rekindling his once-innocent curiosity.

Dr. Raines, standing before the entrance of the ancient and mysterious site, savored that feeling that had once been so familiar to him and remembered the first time he had stepped into a completely untouched tomb in faraway and exotic Egypt.

Only this time, he didn't feel alone. There was a presence, a waiting. As if what slept in the depths had been calling to him all this time.

It wasn't a voice or a whisper, not even a clear thought, but the very air seemed impregnated with an ancient watchfulness. Something below remained latent, not with a defined purpose, but in the way a bottomless well simply is: waiting to be seen.

It wasn't calling him, nor Evelyn, nor any human in particular. It wasn't destiny, but an inevitable fact: what is buried tends to emerge.

And there he was. Perhaps chosen to unravel the secrets dwelling beneath that millennia-old ice, or perhaps just a witness to a presence that required no witnesses. One that had waited without waiting, dreamed without dreaming, under the frozen weight of centuries. One that knew neither haste nor the importance of those who dared disturb its slumber. There was no will there, only existence. An existence so vast and alien that its mere hint was enough to stir the guts of men.

After organizing the equipment they had requested, the two archaeologists descended into the tunnel, followed by a couple of workers carrying the gear. The light from the flashlights danced uncertainly across the rock walls, revealing symbols carved into the stone and strange angles that, in some particular way, guaranteed the tunnel's structural integrity.

"What do you think?" Raines asked, stopping to examine one of the symbols etched with great precision into the rock.

"It doesn't resemble any known writing... except, well, you know, the writing on the tablet," Evelyn replied, cautiously running her fingers over the inscriptions. "It's much older... and more disturbing. It's exactly what we wanted, the tablet is just a small glimpse of a forgotten world."

The group continued descending when suddenly the tunnel opened into an underground chamber. Their flashlights illuminated a vast space, with high ceilings and black stone pillars that seemed to absorb the light whenever it dared to shine on them. In the center of the room stood a massive monolith, bathed in a faint reddish light and covered in the same inscriptions found on the walls. It pulsed gently, as if emitting a barely perceptible rhythmic vibration.

"Holy shit..." Evelyn whispered, unable to look away. "It's impossible," she added, astonished and incredulous. "The place is active... after all this time."

"Yes, like those tortoises that spend years buried and suddenly emerge with all that dirt on their shells. You know? When I was a kid, I had one of those land tortoises, and I remember how, one day, it vanished from my backyard. Naturally, I thought a hawk or something had gotten it. But imagine my surprise when, years later, it reappeared with several centimeters of dirt and grass on its shell."

"We're making history, Evelyn," said Dr. Raines as he walked, somewhat unsteadily, toward the back of the chamber, where another passageway led even deeper into the earth.

As he advanced, he couldn't help but think about the shadowy organization that had recruited him. How was it possible that the brightest scientists and most respected academics lived in complete ignorance? Who the hell knew about this? Was it all a farce? What the hell were all those pompous, clearly clueless professors doing in their offices and digging up pathetic clay pots when someone knew about this? Dr. Raines felt a rage unlike anything he had ever experienced and, at the same time, a profound sense of fortune for not being one of those "pot-hunters."

Evelyn, without a moment's hesitation, followed him. With every step, the shadows grew longer, and the air heavier. The workers, nervous and aware that this was beyond them, exchanged fearful glances before continuing, knowing there was no turning back.

The passage descended at an ever-steeper slope, as if trying to drag them down to the very core of Earth. The sound of their own footsteps echoed off the walls, distorted, as if the echo never fully returned. Raines could feel that reality, as he understood it, was beginning to dissolve. Down below, the laws that governed the surface world seemed to falter.

Despite the cold and the growing pressure of the environment, Evelyn walked with fierce determination. She didn't speak, but her eyes spoke volumes: a mixture of awe and reverence. Raines glanced at her from the corner of his eye and wondered if she, too, had begun to suspect that this discovery far exceeded any comprehension they might possess. That perhaps they weren't unearthing a secret from the past, but opening a door that was never meant to be opened.

The workers, trailing behind, were breathing heavily. One of them whispered a prayer under his breath, something learned in childhood, now surfacing like a lifeline. The other paused briefly, placed a hand on the damp stone wall, and murmured, "This isn't dead… it's just been waiting." But seeing the look his companion gave him, he quickly shook his head, as if trying to convince himself it was just his imagination.

Raines said nothing, but the weight of that sentence weighed heavily on him. Whatever was down there wasn't particularly expecting them. It didn't know them. It couldn't distinguish them, or at least, that was one of the many sensations surfacing within him. But just brushing off the dust of oblivion had been enough to activate it. As if their mere presence had broken an invisible truce between time and whatever lay dormant.

Chapter 3
The Brotherhood

"At last..." a cold, soft woman's voice emerged from the darkness.

"Aren't you afraid?," answered the voice of an old man.

"Of course," she replied, "I'm no fool. But it's been many years of searching, centuries chasing its nearly nonexistent trail."

"And in the end, it's fallen to us to lead the organization at such a crucial moment..."

"Yes, father, in the end it's us. Although sometimes I doubt whether we're really the ones in charge..."

"I understand you. We've seen some things that..."

"Father, what should we do now?"

"Wait..."

"Everything turned out to be true. I have no doubt we'll find what we already know is there."

"Yes."

"Then what are we waiting for?"

An omnipotent silence descended upon the dark room, lit only by the glow of several holographic monitors.

The old man stepped out from the shadows, revealing terrifying eyes without iris or pupil—useless now for those who can see by other means, and approached the computers to open a communication channel.

"It's done. We've found the place. Prepare yourself."

"At last," answered a seductive woman's voice from the other side. "In a few hours, I'll head out with my team to the excavation."

"I can hardly believe she obeys us... I've done terrible things all this time, but Eva gives me chills just hearing her voice."

"I take it we're leaving today?"

"No," the old man replied. "The weather conditions and the long journey there might be too much for my body."

"Not to mention that you're not thrilled about seeing her more than strictly necessary."

"We all pay a price for serving The Brotherhood."

"Yeah... But don't forget we also receive our reward. We don't just pay a price."

"You love bringing up certain topics over and over... More and more, you remind me of her. I don't enjoy many of the things I've had to do, but you're different. You enjoy them..."

"Of course, father. Serving The Brotherhood is a pleasure on every level. Why shouldn't I enjoy carrying out such an honorable task?"

"Because you were human, Mary..."

"Yes, I remember that phase. I've always thought you're too... how should I put it? Moderate..."

"And yet, here I am, the Elder Brother just at the moment when, under my leadership, we've finally found what has eluded discovery for so long. I must have done something right, don't you think?"

"Yes, father, it's clear you've done something right. It's just that many would love to spend more time than necessary in her company when they visit her, and you avoid her like she's a monster."

"Hahaha. She is a monster..."

"Yes, that's true. But so are we... Humanity no longer belongs to us, it only lives in our memories... like an annoying, persistent, unnecessary echo."

"You shouldn't speak that way about your origin."

"Why not? Do you think there's something noble in what we were? A spark of dignity, perhaps?"

"It wasn't all weakness."

"No, of course not. There was also fear, ignorance, arrogance..."

"Do you think we're ready?"

"We are. The world isn't. But it doesn't need us to be ready. The inevitable doesn't require preparation, only a threshold that someone must cross. And that, dear father, is what we're going to do."

Chapter 4
The Labyrinth and the Crystal

In front of them stretched a long tunnel, built from the same porous stone as the strange divans on which they had appeared in that bizarre hemispherical room. Its surface, black and matte, seemed to absorb the faint violet light that still enveloped them, while about fifteen meters ahead, the passageway split into two identical tunnels, equally dark and oppressive.

They all felt it, which isn't to say they were able to describe it... it was as if something were pulling them from the depths of the gallery, as if space itself contracted before them and they were caught and drawn into the void generated by that contraction.

The initial stupor that had paralyzed the group began to fade when Isabel, with an almost obscene calm confidence, stepped forward without hesitation. Without consulting or waiting for approval, she headed toward the tunnel that opened to her right, while her firm steps, echoing against the stone like a mockery of the others' doubts, marked the path everyone should follow. With no clear alternatives and lacking the courage to question her, the rest followed her in silence, hoping the priestess knew what she was doing.

The atmosphere in the tunnel was stifling; the walls, though seemingly smooth, seemed to pulse in unison with a dull heartbeat, as if the place itself were alive. It was then, as they advanced cautiously, that Kolab realized the extraordinary situation did not exempt her from fulfilling her role as a neo-psychoanalyst. It was her duty to maintain the mental stability of the group, and Harun, who walked with unsteady steps and a blank gaze, was clearly the most affected and the one who urgently needed her help.

Projecting as much calm as she could muster, Kolab approached him and in a soft but firm voice asked, "How are you feeling, Harun?" The engineer, surprised by the question, took a few seconds to answer. His broken, trembling voice barely rose above the echo of their footsteps, "Fine... I guess..."

Kolab gave him a kind though forced smile, aware that any gesture of support could be crucial. "It's okay to feel scared. We all feel out of place here (she couldn't help thinking that wasn't so true for Isabel), but we're in this together. If you ever feel the need to talk, I'm here."

Harun nodded weakly but didn't reply. He appreciated the gesture, although Kolab's words didn't ease the knot of terror tightening in his chest. Meanwhile, Isabel pressed on, her silhouette standing out against the distant yet close glow of the purple light that seemed to emanate from the elusive heart of the place and from wherever one cast their gaze.

Kolab looked around with growing unease, the feeling that something invisible was watching them began to seep deep into her being, and though she said nothing, she knew the others felt it too.

The group's silence was not merely caution: it was pure fear.

"It's curious, thought Kolab as she watched Harun. Once again I see how the illusion of control we humans tend to project onto the world around us collapses in the face of the mysterious unfolding of the most unexpected events that burst into our lives, without warning, without asking permission... And yet, we humans are incapable of accepting that seemingly primordial chaos that governs everything. We are incapable of understanding that the small branch carried by the river's current does not govern the current itself nor, consequently, its own course..."

It happened as if by chance, as if that very current she had been thinking about, to confirm her view, brought along another surprise, this time in the form of a strange memory. It was with the greatest astonishment that, as she timidly advanced through the dark passage, her agitated mind slid into an unfamiliar room where, recalling a situation she had never experienced, she perceived herself as if she were Harun, who, terrified and as a child, had been savagely beaten by his father. The man had entered the room blaming Harun for something that hadn't been his fault in any way, something about a plate of food that should have been in the fridge but wasn't. Harun's father didn't even let give the boy a chance to explain himself. He brought his closed fist down on him with extreme violence.

Stupefied, Kolab lived the scene as if it were her own memory and could do nothing but shudder at the overwhelming sadness that invaded Harun—and now her. In that dark room, more than the physical integrity of a child had been lost: the shadow of absolute horror and the cruelest helplessness covered everything, drowning out any attempt to make sense of such abuse.

Kolab, cold as she was, her eyes soaking with Harun's grief, realized that she hadn't cried in decades, and bewildered, and stunned, tried to regain control.

After experiencing this moment of vulnerability, both foreign and personal, she wondered about the very nature of the event and assumed it must have been a product of the suggestion that the damned place was exerting on her mind.

The group continued forward, following Isabel's firm and determined lead, as she chose the path through that unusual place without hesitation. The surroundings revealed themselves as a stony labyrinth that swallowed the crew of the *Persephone*, drawing them deeper and deeper into its unfathomable depths, which seemed to hold some kind of fascinating secret that Isabel yearned to uncover.

How long had they been walking? the Captain wondered, when he noticed Harun, with a fearful expression, staring at him. Just as Diop was about to confront him inquisitively, the priestess suddenly stopped in front of something that overwhelmed them all.

Something that could in no way be there.

Diop gulped in shock and rubbed his eyes in disbelief: before them lay a gigantic abyssal chasm of insane proportions, able of containing the labyrinth thanks to some spatial anomaly beyond all Euclidean comprehension. None of them would have been able to explain it. It was obvious that something of that magnitude should have been perceived from the moment they entered the place, and yet such a colossus of emptiness had appeared suddenly, as if it could have been hidden behind a simple wall.

What contained what, the labyrinth the chasm, or the chasm the labyrinth?

They all wondered this in a vain attempt to explain what they were seeing, as their hearts were cloaked in insignificance.

As if held by the very place itself by threads as invisible as the void, an enormous black crystal floated some ten meters above their heads. Its seemingly infinite and shifting facets reflected moments from each of their pasts. It was Aukan who, dizzy from the insane vision, collapsed, completely disoriented, against the hard, porous stone floor.

The others also fell almost immediately, after seeing their own pasts reflected in the infinite sides of the crystal. As they fell, they experienced some of those events for what seemed like hours or days.

Diop, completely overwhelmed, saw himself running desperately through immensely long corridors identical to those of the *Persephone* but much larger. He seemed to be searching for something with an obsessive urgency: his memories, his past lost somewhere in the depths of those cursed corridors.

"Where are you, Father?" Diop exclaimed, searching among the violet reflections for a glimmer of true golden light. "Who the hell am I?! What is my name?!"

The experience was no less traumatic for Harun, who, terrified and emitting bloodcurdling moans and screams that echoed through the macabre labyrinth, was forced to relive and immerse himself in the terrible beating his father gave him as a child, one that had left him on the brink of death. Only this time, his father wasn't alone: his mother was there too, actively participating in the abuse.

For her part, Kolab had to face her greatest fear: feeling.

Paralyzed before Harun, she experienced what it would be like to merge with him into a single body, overwhelmed by the intense emotions of that pathetic little man. She cried inconsolably as if someone else's pain had taken over her being. Each tear that fell seemed to drag with it a piece of the anguish Harun felt from being rejected again and again.

She intensely experienced the same frustrations he had suffered since childhood which continued as, immersed in the cold and cruel machinery of social networks, his attempts to seduce the women behind those cold profiles were constantly ignored or rejected. She could feel the weight of his despair, that helplessness that grew with each unanswered message in that sea of virtual profiles offering nothing but emptiness and disappointment.

The pain of humiliation grew palpable in her chest, and Kolab, unable to help it, lived those emotions as if they were her own, as if Harun's pain had left indelible marks on her soul. That loneliness enveloped her as Harun's longing for connection and affection transformed into a silent scream that resonated within her, only to be answered by the dull echo of herself.

"How can someone feel so much pain and still survive?" she wondered, as time and again, Harun, or rather, she herself, was rejected and ignored by all those women who, smiling from the other side of the ethereal holographic screen, seemed to mock her and her ridiculous attempts to seduce them.

The experience was no more forgiving for Aukan. The hitman, 123 years old but with a youthful appearance thanks to longevity treatments, was facing a crucial moment in his life: Pluto's opposition to his natal position[1].

During his experience with the crystal, Aukan found himself in a devastated mindscape, a cold, empty space where the echoes of his crimes resonated endlessly. Each murder, each life taken, manifested as a shadow that surrounded and accused him. For the first time, he felt a crushing guilt. It was as if the voices of his

---

[1] It's important to clarify at this point that, at the beginning of the 21st century, the development of A.I. led to the conclusion that synchronicity is a real phenomenon. To this end, both the history of humanity and that of a large number of people were analyzed. Synchronicity was described by C.G. Jung, a renowned psychoanalyst born in the 19th century. He defined the phenomenon as "a temporal coincidence of two or more events related to each other in a non-causal manner, the meaningful content of which is the same or similar for the subject experiencing it." It is a completely real phenomenon that lies beyond what is considered probabilistically feasible. That is, human subjects, throughout their lives, experience an "X" number of situations that are beyond what is probabilistically acceptable but hold a profound meaning for each of them. It was as a result of this that other issues were discovered, such as the fact that tarot works by transcending these probabilistic limits by manifesting a synchronous discourse beyond chance. The same thing also happened with astrology.

During the crisis that every human experiences when Pluto passes through the diametrically opposite point where the planetoid had been at the time of the individual's birth (the "opposition"), those affected are irrevocably confronted by their own darkness. It is as if it manifests before them in the form of seemingly acausal events and experiences, yet intimately linked to each individual's spiritual reality.

victims formed a chorus of wails that permeated his mind and being, soaking his hardened heart, softening it and forcing him to feel guilt.

In that moment of painful introspection, he realized that his soul, which he had always believed nonexistent, not only existed but was rotten and undone by the weight of his actions. A feeling of irremediable loss flooded him, and he felt that all that remained of him was an empty shell. The hitman, who had always been cold and calculating, discovered that even the most callous creature could not escape the judgment of his own humanity.

For her part, Isabel, so self-assured as she advanced with firm determination through the labyrinth, came face to face with a dire reality she would never have to find in that place. The crystal, with its cruel and lucid impartiality, projected a vision that tore her soul apart: a life that could have been.

There she was, not as a devotee of the Dark Mother but as a healer, a guide who offered hope and relief to others. In this alternative version of her existence, Isabel saw how her life intertwined with the luminous and compassionate paths offered by other philosophies of life. She found herself surrounded by grateful faces, by communities thriving under her care, and by an inner peace she had never experienced before, a product of the genuine gratitude projected upon her by strangers who, nevertheless, seemed to harbor sincere love and respect for her.

The contrast with her real life was unbearable. The Isabel who gazed into the crystal felt bitterness and regret growing within her like an unstoppable tide. Her devotion, which she had once believed to be her greatest strength, now revealed to her as her greatest condemnation; with each second, the crystal made it clear that it was her choice, her mistake, that had brought her to this point of no return. And to make matters worse, Isabel felt the presence of the goddess in her mind, an inhuman force that seemed to mock her regret.

"Did you think you could run away from the truth?" The voice echoed in her mind resonating in h the depths of her inner labyrinth. The labyrinth outside her, meanwhile, seemed to resonate with a primordial laughter, as Isabel, consumed by grief, fell to her knees.

Facing the black crystal, each member of the group was undone. That vision had shown them that the power trapping them was not only overwhelmingly superior, but also knew and exploited their deepest fears and wounds. The stone abyss they found themselves in, now more than ever, seemed ready to devour them whole.

Kolab was the first to react after the terrible experience, and to everyone's surprise, including herself, she did so by physically assaulting Harun. Her eyes reddened from crying and her lost gaze in thought, she stood before him and slapped him hard, repeatedly, until Harun seemed to react.

"Did you think you could hide who you are, you piece of shit?" she yelled in his face as she swung at him again with an open hand.

"I... I don't know what you're talking about," Harun stammered, overwhelmed both by his experience with the crystal and by Kolab's sudden fury.

"Of course you do, you damn idiot!" she replied, beside herself, blaming him for what she'd just experienced.

"Enough!" Diop intervened, still dazed but with a firm voice. "We can't lose control! We have to stay calm. We must survive this damn place!"

The Captain's order had no time to calm the mood, because at that precise moment Isabel burst into a raucous, hysterical laugh that left everyone speechless. It was such an unexpected reaction from her, who had always displayed a firm attitude since their arrival, that no one knew how to react.

For a few endless seconds, no one dared to speak to her. It was, once again, Captain Diop who attempted to regain control of the situation.

"Isabel! What the hell are you doing?" he demanded sternly.

Isabel suddenly stopped laughing, lifted her gaze, and locked her demented eyes on the Captain's. In the tense silence that followed, everyone held their breath, as if the air itself had stopped, trying to acquire the weight of the stone for itself. Finally, she broke the silence with a whisper:

"She shows no mercy, neither for those who blindly obey her designs, nor for those of us who raised her children."

"What... what did she say?" Harun murmured, visibly frightened.

"Nothing," Diop replied sharply. "Nothing that matters. Now, get up. We must move forward if we want to get out of this place alive."

One by one, the group members got to their feet, all except Aukan, who remained curled up on the ground in a fetal position, silently crying. His mind was a whirlwind, and the anguish only kept growing wildly inside him.

"Is what I saw real?" he kept asking himself. "Do I have a soul, or is this place just playing with my mind, exploiting my guilt as a kind of attack?" He tried to convince himself it was all an illusion, just another tool of this place to break his resistance. "I never had a soul," he thought vehemently, "just moments of weakness. I can't let this damn place defeat me."

"Aukan!" Diop shouted, finally pulling him from his state.

Little by little, Aukan got up, his gaze still lost, but confusedly answering to his Captain's call.

After the experience, and with no one daring to look at the menacing crystal still floating above their heads, they advanced in silence through one of the tunnels. This time, they followed Diop's firm pace, who, though deeply distressed, did not allow his emotions to cloud his mind or become evident to his crew.

The atmosphere was heavy, filled with tension and fear. After a few minutes walking in silence, Kolab, now somewhat calmer, gathered the courage to break the silence.

"What did you see?" she asked Isabel directly.

The priestess took a moment to respond, fixing an unreadable gaze on Kolab before answering curtly:

"And you?"

Kolab hesitated, but finally responded sincerely, still reflecting the weight of what she had experienced.

"So you experienced a fusion with Harun... and felt his frustration as if it were your own, with an intensity that transcends your own feelings," speculated Isabel, in a tone more reflective than understanding. "Interesting... It could be a test from the goddess, a challenge to prove we're up to the task."

The slight tremor in her voice revealed that not even she was entirely convinced of her own words.

"I don't think this is a test," Diop interjected, his voice deep and firm. "I think this place is rejecting us."

"It doesn't matter," Aukan said decisively, now mentally recovered. "We must stay strong. We cannot allow this place to defeat us."

"It won't," Diop responded with determination, feigning a strength he perhaps didn't fully feel.

The group continued forward in silence, but Isabel didn't let much time pass before launching another question.

"And you, Aukan? What did you see?"

Aukan did not answer. His silence was more eloquent than any word.

Tension once again enveloped the group as they walked through the endless corridors. The dim purple light illuminating them seemed, at times, to take on a strange watery appearance, rippling like the surface of a restless lake.

Chapter 5
Entangled

Dr. Raines's trembling legs moved forward as if asking permission from the ground beneath their feet, fearful no longer of God, but perhaps of something older. Something that, at least in part, still retained some operational capacity to this day.

"How is it possible, Evelyn, that no one in the universities knew anything about all this? How can it be that right now, in Egypt, doctors who are supposed to be the spearhead of world archaeological research are digging in search of the umpteenth shitty tomb?"

"It's obvious there's a shadow government that has gone much further than we could have ever suspected..."

"It's all a farce."

"No, not all. This is no farce, this place is real... And we have been chosen to uncover it."

"That's true, Evelyn, but... this situation overwhelms me. I can't stop thinking about some of our colleagues, blindly trusting a paradigm that is just a hoax to keep the population obedient and ignorant."

"What do you think would happen if all this came to light?"

"I don't know, but ignorance is worse than knowledge. Of that I'm sure."

"Yes… I believe that too. Or well, at least I used to. Now I might be starting to harbor some doubts about it… I'm not sure our societies could bear the weight of this truth."

"Well, I'm sure many couldn't, but I don't think that would be a problem for them; I think they'd go on just as they are, believing in nonsense, empty religions, lying politicians, watching trashy TV and believing what really matters is a pathetic football team."

"It's sad, but I think, deep down, you're right. Releasing this truth would simply widen the gap that separates some humans from others."

"Exactly, the brave ones would move forward and the sheep would remain locked in their pens. The time will come when the former will be able to leave Earth in marvelous spaceships and leave the flock behind forever."

"I'm betting on it. If only…"

The angular tunnel, bathed in the distinctive red light that ruled the place and describing a downward spiral, delved ever deeper into the ancient valley, as if suggesting to the explorers that such depth was not only physical, but also reflected, in some peculiar way, the unfathomable depths of their own minds, where equally ancient mysteries lay hidden. After descending for just over half an hour and finding themselves more than a kilometer deep, they found themselves before a fork that, at least for the moment, seemed to mark the end of their descent.

"And now?" asked Michael, one of the workers.

"We'll go for the one on the left one first," ordered Dr. Raines.

"Alright," replied the worker, struggling to pronounce those two words clearly to prevent his terror from becoming too evident.

"Look at that," Raines pointed with his flashlight, his voice full of excitement.

In front of them, a wide gallery of a strange reddish metallic rock, different from the rest of the structure, reflected the red light with an effect reminiscent of a psychedelic scene from a seventies sci-fi film.

"It's a mining operation. Look at those machines and the pointed mechanical arms that emerge from them. And those containers: some of them still contain rocks extracted from the walls."

"Yes, you're right, Evelyn. Despite their vaguely skeletal and organic appearance, those devices are clearly what you're saying; they're so strange, so alien to any design ever made by a human being..."

"They remind me of the work of a 20th century artist, Giger or something like that his name was."

"No idea, Evelyn. Aside from that, it's also quite strange that I have absolutely no clue what mineral this part of the cavern could be composed of. It's supposed to be terrestrial, how is it possible we don't know?"

"Yes, same here, I've never seen anything like it either, not to mention the unusual metal those machines are made of."

Hours passed before the group was certain that, at least in the path they had taken after completing the spiral descent to the fork, there were only galleries dedicated to the extraction of the strange mineral. It was then that they decided it was time to return to the surface to rest and wait for a new day, during which they would explore the other tunnel.

"What do you think, Doctor?"

"I don't know... It's evident that a civilization predating humanity was here extracting that mineral. However, it also seems clear that the site's function wasn't limited solely to mining. The inscriptions on the walls seem to speak of a reality that, clearly, goes beyond something purely industrial."

"That's what I thought. I have a feeling that the other corridor harbors secrets in its depths that surpass anything we've seen today."

"That's true… I don't know what to expect. What we saw today has already been the most mind-blowing experience of my life."

"I say the same, Doctor. It's an absolute honor to be part of your team, even if it's hard for me to process all of this."

That night, after uploading the new data into the camp computers and briefing the rest of the team, Raines and Evelyn were forced to take sleeping pills despite their exhaustion. Their excitement was so intense that it was impossible for them to sleep; the images they had witnessed during the descent, burned into their memories, resurfaced again and again from the depths of their minds, stubbornly activating their tired brains.

During their sleep, they experienced strange visions of the tunnels and that hypnotic red light. From it, blurry, emerged a series of monstrous, tentacled creatures that, as if coming from a distant and forgotten past, tried to keep the place safe from prying eyes.

"Good morning, Doctor… It's been a strange night. I had some disturbing dreams… There were some beings in the tunnels, stalking me, they seemed to want to scare me away from the place…"

"Really? I dreamed the same thing. They had strange spherical heads covered in tentacles, right? How is that possible?"

"I don't know. We have to keep in mind that we are completely unaware of the nature of the place and the technology it houses. Could it be some kind of phenomenon similar to quantum entanglement?"

"It could be… There are inconclusive studies linking that phenomenon to certain deeper aspects of consciousness. Perhaps our minds have somehow became linked because we were together during the descent. I know it sounds crazy, but given what we've seen, I no longer feel capable of rule anything out, no matter how far-fetched it may seem at first."

"I wonder if the same thing happened to the workers who accompanied us… Let's go wake them up."

When they arrived at the tent where the technical staff was sleeping, they found Andrew having breakfast, but Michael was not there.

"Where's Michael?" Evelyn asked Andrew.

"Isn't he in bed? I haven't seen him... I thought he was still sleeping. I haven't rested well, I had some strange dreams, I haven't been very aware of what was happening around me this morning. Besides, I just woke up and my head feels like a professional batter was practicing with it like a baseball..."

"Tell me about those dreams, Andrew."

"Well... I was down there, in the tunnels, and there was something there. Something watching me, but... I don't know, I can't remember what it was. I just remember not wanting to go down, I was really scared."

"Evelyn, come out quickly!" Dr. Raines's voice cut through the silence. "Out here there are footprints leading away, as if someone decided to leave the camp and venture into the white void."

"Oh, my God..." Evelyn exclaimed, hurrying to join him. Seeing with her own eyes the trail leading away from the tent into the hostile and frozen vastness sent a shiver down her spine.

"I bet my neck that trail leads to the ruins..."

"You think so, Doctor?"

"Yes..."

Chapter 6
Lost

"I think we've been through here before," Harun stated cautiously, breaking the silence with his uncertain voice.

"Oh really?" Diop replied curtly, without stopping.

"Well... maybe not. It's just that everything looks so similar here..." Harun tried to correct himself, hesitating as he crossed his arms and looked down at the floor, as if hiding.

"I also think this is the second time we've been through this place," Isabel chimed in, her tone blunt and direct. "We should have turned left at the last fork."

"Goddammit! Will you all just shut the fuck up?" Diop snapped, deeply exasperated, stopping in his tracks and glaring at the group with a blazing gaze.

At that precise moment, Diop was drawn into a strange and unsettling memory, as alien as it was familiar. He saw himself, but somehow knew he was Kolab, arriving for the first time at the center where she had studied neopsychoanalysis. The scene was vivid: the white hallways, the omnipresent silence, the faint anxiety of a novice thumping in the chest. But how did he know this? Why was he remembering it? The questions swirled in his mind, finding no satisfactory answers, as the "memory" unfolded in his own mind as if it had always been there.

The change in his expression did not go unnoticed. His companions watched him closely with concern.

"Are you okay?" Kolab asked, noticing his blank stare.

"Yes, yes..." Diop shook his head as if trying to dispel a cloud. "Just... a slight dizziness, nothing major. Let's move on."

The silhouettes of the five crew members stood out against the dim and watery violet glow that bathed the twisted place. Only the echo of their footsteps broke the oppressive silence, a constant reminder of the solitude that reigned there.

Suddenly, Harun spoke again, his voice trembling:

"I'm sure we've been through here before..."

Diop stopped, this time fully aware that the statement was true. He looked around, observing the repetitive details on the walls, and placed one of his large hands on the rough surface. He exhaled, nodding slowly.

"We should go back and take the tunnel to the left at the last fork," Harun suggested, this time a little more firmly.

Diop nodded again without saying a word, leading the group in the opposite direction. One by one, the five crew members of the *Persephone* advanced silently toward the tunnel Harun had indicated.

With each step, the uncertainty and tension grew. The labyrinth seemed endless, a living enigma playing with their senses. But despite everything, they held onto a vague hope that, around one of the many corners, they would finally find a way out.

"It's a test," Isabel thought, trying to convince herself of it. "I know her. She won't let the unworthy succeed, she won't let them survive... It's fine, it's the right thing to do, I understand, Mother. Many succumb and only a few are accepted, I understand that very well," she told herself, her mind drifting away from the place, away from herself.

"I love you, Marc. I'm so glad I met you," a relaxed, young Isabel whispered to the figure lying next to her, smoking, in the bed of the quaint bamboo-wood hotel they had visited during a summer vacation in their university days.

"I love you too, Isabel," he replied with a calm smile. "You know I love studying, that I've worked really hard… but I could stay here forever, diving, fishing… I'm sure we'd do just fine."

"I don't believe you," she laughed. "You wouldn't last two months living like a hippie fisherman. That's not you, Marc, and you know that very well. Besides, I hate hippies," Isabel laughed.

"You're right," he laughed back. "I couldn't stand it. Anyway, we have four days left. Although h it's obvious neither of us could stay here much longer without going crazy, I'm going to enjoy them as much as I can," said Marc as he put out the joint he'd been smoking and closed… Kolab's? mouth with a long kiss.

"What the hell…?" she thought, giving Isabel a questioning look.

"What is it?" asked Isabel, forgetting Marc and returning to the labyrinth.

"Marc…"

Surprised, Isabel didn't know what to say. That was one of her most cherished memories, one she didn't want to share with anyone. It was hers. Only hers.

Kolab sensed what Isabel was feeling from her reaction. Embarrassed, she said nothing more and kept walking; she had never seen anything like that cross the priestess's face…

"It can't be. We got it wrong again. We've ended up in the same place," said a distressed Harun.

"Goddammit…" Kolab clenched her jaw in intense frustration. "From now on, I'll keep my right hand on this wall. We won't leave the wall. We'll follow it to the end."

The others nodded and followed her in funereal silence.

"We've been walking for quite a while. I don't feel hungry or thirsty. It's like fatigue doesn't affect me in this place," an increasingly bewildered Diop stated.

"And it doesn't," replied Isabel, cryptic.

"What is this place, witch?"

"For you, this space is a kind of non-place."

"What?"

"Places have meaning. A place isn't just a space devoid of function."

"Shit, what the fuck does that even mean?"

"A non-place is an empty space, devoid of identity for those who pass through it. Think of an airport or a waiting room. You're not there to stay; you just pass through."

Diop still didn't fully understand, and she continued:

"But there are other kinds of non-places. Places that once had meaning, but for those who visit now, are just stage sets. Like the pyramids of Egypt: their true purpose has been lost to tourists, who see them as just another attraction. They don't care about the original meaning, they just use them as backgrounds for their Instagram photos."

"The difference," a somber Harun pointed out, "is that in this place or space, call it what you will, what reigns is not the emptiness left by its former inhabitants, like in the pyramids of Egypt. Here, there is something else."

"Exactly," Isabel confirmed, amused. "And I'm afraid whatever lives in this place can't stand tourists."

"It's a matter of respect," Harun concluded surprisingly, exchanging a dark glance with her.

Chapter 7
The Descent

"You were right, Doctor, the trail leads to the underground complex. I don't understand…"

"I think that, somehow, those shared dreams mean something profound. They are the embodiment of a change, of something that happened to us or occurred within us yesterday."

"I don't understand. What do you mean?"

"That we can't pretend nothing happened after three people who descended into that place had the same dream. A prepared mind must detect the anomaly and react before the situation gets out of control. Otherwise, it will be the situation that controls us."

"I see… What do you think we should do?"

"Go down. As soon as possible. We have to find that poor man."

The descent, this time, felt shorter for Evelyn, Raines, and Andrew. Or at least, so they thought it was. For Olivia, Michael's replacement, however, it was agony. Every step she took in those dark tunnels felt like a fall into eternity. Sweat soaked her underwear beneath the safety suit, and her legs trembled with every meter. But she couldn't turn back. She needed this job. The money was worth it, and if someone had to be replaced, then she had to do it to the best of her ability.

What she didn't know was that she would never get out of that place… nor earn a single cent.

"Where did he go?" Evelyn murmured.

"I'd bet not toward the mine. Don't ask me why, but I know. Michael didn't go that way. Follow me!"

They advanced cautiously until they reached and crossed the threshold they hadn't crossed yesterday, leaving the relative safety of the tunnel behind. Then they saw it.

Evelyn was speechless. Breathless. Her mouth hung open and her eyes wide as full moons, unable to process what was before her.

The pyramid-shaped room, about thirty meters high, with a square base measuring twenty meters per side, wasn't what most unsettled her, since a red and black trapezoid, floating in the center, emitted pulses of red light, luminous pulses that seemed to sync with the breathing of those present. However, the most disturbing thing was the walls. Or rather, what was visible through them.

They were transparent, almost invisible, and beyond them, as if in an impossible geometry, other pyramidal chambers were repeated. In each one, motionless, rising in sepulchral silence, stood enormous "trees." They weren't actually trees, but rather black, twisted masses, creatures with an erratic morphology from whose trunks emerged gnarled "branches" that seemed to fold upon themselves in a dance frozen in time.

"Those are the beings from the cave paintings…" Evelyn murmured.

"So it seems…" Raines replied, his gaze fixed on those abominations.

"They are not from this world..." Evelyn whispered before collapsing to her knees, tears streaming down her face.

"Oh my God, don't come any closer, Doctor!" Andrew shouted.

"We did it," Raines declared, taking slow steps toward the transparent wall, ignoring Andrew's warning.

Raines stood before the invisible barrier and observed, fascinated, the creature that rose behind it. It was immense, imposing. It didn't move, but its skin pulsed with an impossible life; its shape obeyed no natural logic. Every moment of observation distanced it further from the concept of a tree. Its branches were organic, bulbous, twisted masses, as if nature itself had erred in shaping it. The doctor swallowed hard, disgusted, astonished. And, to his misfortune, completely enthralled. At that moment, guided by an unconscious impulse, he reached out to place his hand on the wall. To his surprise, it offered no resistance, and his hand passed right through.

"Doctor, be careful," said a fearful Evelyn as, for some strange reason, she nervously checked the strap of her watch.

Raines didn't reply and, without hesitation, stepped into the chamber where the enormous creature seemed to remain "frozen." For some reason, he remembered Michael, and while taking some photos of the horrible entity, he questioned himself about the fate of that poor man.

"Doctor," whispered a terrified Andrew, "don't you think we're taking too big a risk? We were supposed to come down to look for Michael... He's obviously not here, right? Don't you think we should go back?

"I think Andrew is right," Olivia agreed, her words slurring, gripped by the overwhelming impression the creatures had on her.

"Wait a moment," Evelyn insisted. "I'm sure the doctor will return once he's photographed the creature. Then we'll ascend to the surface, don't worry.

Olivia wouldn't have been able to say why—perhaps it was something in her tone of voice, perhaps a subtle tremor born of insecurity—but she didn't believe a single word that came, lamely, from Evelyn's mouth.

Unfortunately for all of them, none of them noticed that one of the creatures had begun to move slightly in one of the chambers behind them.

None of them were fortunate enough to see one of those "branches" begin to move lazily, resembling more a black, wrinkled tentacle than anything of arboreal appearance.

Meanwhile, Doctor Raines continued taking photos, circling the motionless creature. Some images captured large sections of its surface, while others sought to document the smallest details and textures of its skin.

In contrast to his excitement, tension grew among the other members of the group, who didn't dare cross the transparent wall behind which the doctor and the creature stood.

"Please, let's get out of here," Olivia sobbed. "I can't take it anymore, something bad is going to happen, I'm sure of it."

"Wait, damn it!" Evelyn snapped at her with a mixture of terror and severity.

Then, Olivia felt something behind her. She didn't need to see it to understand what was there. She screamed. She screamed like she never screamed before.

Chapter 8
Ego

Kolab was aware that, given her age, she was experiencing her first Pluto opposition to her natal Pluto and, obviously, she did not miss the irony that fate had, somehow, sent her precisely to Pluto. She wasn't a superstitious person, but certain thoughts inevitably emerged from her subconscious. After all, she was fully aware that some of the discoveries made by A.I. in analyzing massive amounts of data in recent times were proving that concepts like synchronicity[2] and disciplines like astrology held truths that, although uncomfortable for many, were beginning to be indisputable. While much research remained to be done, particularly regarding the exact relationship and the intensity of the bond between astral dance and the human mind, it was evident that, at least at the level of world events and personal life, there was an undeniable connection.

---

[2] Synchronicity (sin-, from the Greek συν-, union, and χρόνος, time) is the term chosen by Carl Gustav Jung to refer to "the simultaneity of two events linked by meaning for an individual but in an acausal manner."

On the other hand, Kolab possessed a remarkable knowledge of Greco-Roman mythology, so she couldn't help but wonder about the dark figure of Hades-Pluto, the legendary god of the underworld. She tried to recall those cases where a mortal, after entering the realm of death, had managed to return to the world of the living. Unfortunately, there weren't many of them, and all had paid a high price: Orpheus, the mythical poet, lost Eurydice due to his impatience; Heracles accepted that not even he could escape his fate; Theseus was trapped and, after being rescued, found only the loss of his people's favor; Odysseus witnessed the suffering of souls and the death of his own mother; Psyche experienced the pain of self- discovery before transcending...

Leading the group, lost in these thoughts, trying to find some clue that might be useful, she suddenly noticed an alien memory seeping into her mind from somewhere unknown. This time, she saw herself as a merciless Aukan, leaving several members of her team behind in a jungle, hoping they would be captured or eliminated by the enemy, thus creating a window of opportunity to save her own life.

"How is this possible?" she wondered as she moved forward, her right hand resting against the wall. I'm not experiencing it as something alien... it truly as if I've lived it, as if my ego were permeable to the memories of others."

Implanting memories was not something human science, despite all the science fiction stories, was anywhere near to achieving. Kolab felt a stirring of distrust begin to creep in inside her. What did the others know about her? Which of her memories were no longer hers alone?

At that moment, something interrupted the frantic stream of her mind. In front of her, for no more than two seconds, a fleeting image appeared, only to vanish as suddenly as it had burst into her field of vision.

They all saw it: a blurry, pinkish figure that, in part, reminded them of a winged crustacean. Its spherical head, covered in tentacles, seemed to turn toward them in that brief instant, as if, somehow, it had seen them too.

Kolab screamed and backed away until he collided with Captain Diop, who, still in shock, stopped her retreat with his firm hands.

"What the fuck was that?" exclaimed an incredulous Aukan.

"We call them Mi-Go," Isabel replied.

"What?!" the Captain inquired.

"Mi-Go," Isabel insisted. "They're cosmic beings, aliens... They came to the solar system eons ago from the distant Ross 508 system, which they reached after a long journey from the unknown depths of the cosmos."

Harun felt an overwhelming urge to cry. How had he ended up in this place? Why did he always have such bad luck? How was it possible his life could be so miserable? He asked himself over and over again: Why me?

"We must remain calm," Isabel intervened. "I'm convinced this is a test. My goddess is very demanding; she doesn't accept just anyone. It's something you have to deserve."

"And how the hell do you know so many things, damn witch?" Harun spat the words with extreme hostility.

At that moment, an alien memory assailed him. He saw himself, as Isabel, handing over a human baby to one of those Mi-Go on a dark mountaintop, where several megaliths rose imposingly from a thick purple mist, exactly the same hue as the watery light of the labyrinth. The horror of the vision overwhelmed him and he collapsed to the ground, screaming:

"We can't go on like this," Aukan said. "If we let this fucking coward keep dragging us down, we'll never get out of here."

"Sure, let's do what you did with your battalion mates in that jungle, right, Aukan? Let's leave him behind to buy time while the enemy takes care of him," Kolab said coldly.

"What?" muttered a stunned Aukan.

"Don't play dumb. I remember it too," Isabel added with a smug smile.

Aukan, red with rage, advanced toward Isabel, but Diop stepped between them shouting:

"Enough! Can't you see this place wants to tear us apart? We have to stick together. We only have each other, goddamn it!"

"The Captain is right," Kolab agreed. "This place attacks our minds, and we can't let it divide us or drive us mad. We must stand firm against whatever lies ahead."

"Harun, you need to pull yourself together, for fuck's sake," Diop said in a firm but warm tone. "We need you at one hundred percent. This is hard for all of us, but we can't let this place consume us."

"I saw what she did," Harun murmured. "She gave a baby to one of those creatures. She's part of this…"

"That doesn't matter now. I'm afraid none of us are saints here. What matters is getting the hell out of this labyrinth and going home. Got it?"

"Listen to the Captain, Harun," Isabel said with her icy voice. "Sometimes you have to do horrible things to advance along your own path. That's all it is…"

Harun looked at her with a mix of fear and contempt. Then he nodded with resignation at Diop and, without saying another word, prepared to keep walking, frustrated and terrified by the ominous situation he was trapped in.

The group resumed their march. Once again, their silhouettes dissolved into the watery purple light, like shadows of a distant memory fading before an implacable and hostile fate that no longer had a place for them. Step by step, they ventured into the unfathomable depths of its gloomy interior.

"Explain that 'non-place' thing to me again," Diop asked, his brow furrowed and his voice laden with barely concealed impatience.

Isabel looked at him with a mixture of indifference and boredom.

"The way I see it," she began, letting her words slide out slowly, "a space isn't truly a place until a consciousness gives it meaning. Without that, it's just a void. Tell me, Captain...," her tone became almost maternal, with a thinly veiled biting irony, "what does this space mean to you?"

The silence that followed was more revealing than any answer. Diop lowered his gaze, unable to find a retort that didn't sound ridiculous even in his own head. Isabel's smile, languid and self-satisfied, quickly appeared. It wasn't pure cruelty, but a kind of pity tinged with contempt, as if she saw in him something hopelessly limited. In her mind, it was clear: someone with such a mediocre level of awareness would never be worthy of being accepted into one of the dwellings of Shub-Niggurath.

"You could give this space a new meaning, if that's important to you," Kolab interjected, her soft voice contrasting with Isabel's coldness.

Diop looked up, caught between curiosity and suspicion. Something in those words stirred an unease he had tried to bury.

"And what the hell is that supposed to mean?" he snapped, with a tone more defensive than defiant.

Kolab remained unmoved.

"It means," Isabel said, seizing the answer as if it belonged to her, "that you could find meaning in what's happening to you here if you manage to integrate it into the story you tell yourself about yourself. But..." her eyes gleamed with a malicious glint, "I doubt it will be easy. People like you tend to fill their personal story with exaggerations, small acts of fanciful heroism, and an inflated sense of importance that has nothing to do with reality."

Those words cut deeper than Diop would have liked to admit. For an instant, his mask of arrogance wavered, revealing a crack of doubt. Kolab noticed, but chose not to intervene, knowing there were inner battles that could only be fought alone.

"It's not about being a hero" she added finally, in an attempt to build a bridge. "It's about accepting that this place can be part of who you are. Or who you fear to be. Understand that this isn't a fragment of reality separate from you. Now, this labyrinth is already part of you."

Isabel watched in silence, amused. Diop, for his part, looked away, feeling that, for the first time, the walls of the space he occupied weren't the only thing suffocating him.

Chapter 9
Eva

Eva calmly descended from the helicopter that had flown her from Anchorage, Alaska's most populous city, to the excavation site. The welcome, delivered by a violent icy blizzard, seemed absolutely fitting for anyone who had had the opportunity to look directly into her icy blue eyes. Her boots sank into the snow with a muffled crunch as she moved forward without haste, leaving pilot behind, who watched her silhouette with a mixture of fascination and fear.

All around her, the makeshift camp rose up out of mist and ice, with tents and metal structures half-buried in frost. A group of archaeologists and workers awaited her arrival with obvious trepidation. Eva scanned them with her eyes, as if assessing the usefulness of each one while she licked her lips with concealed hunger.

"So, neither the doctors nor the workers have returned from their incursion into the site in search of the guy who, for reasons unknown, went in alone without informing anyone, is that correct?" Her voice was clear and firm, without a hint of concern.

"Yes, ma'am," one of the archaeologists replied, intimidated by Eva's absolute beauty. His voice trembled just barely. "They went down about seven hours ago."

"I see," she nodded, distractedly playing with her long bluish-white hair. "What did you say your name was?"

"Arthur, ma'am. My name is Arthur," he said, lost in the crystalline waters of her eyes.

"Very well, Arthur. Would you like to accompany me into the structure? I need someone to carry some equipment, but I'd prefer not to take a simple worker. You see, I like a brain behind strong arms, and you seem to possess both qualities…"

Arthur swallowed hard. The mere idea of entering that place terrified him, but Eva's invitation felt like an order disguised as flattery. His instincts screamed at him to refuse, to find an excuse, but his will was overwhelmed by the woman's magnetic presence. Unable to do otherwise, he nodded.

Shortly after, Arthur found himself carrying the equipment Eva had indicated. His mind plunged into the most aberrant sexual fantasies he could imagine, inspired by her otherworldly beauty. He didn't think of his wife, he didn't remember his children. Nothing could compare to that woman. Arthur knew he was lost. What was he going to do now? He couldn't return to his normal life; nothing would satisfy him anymore. Only Eva.

The descent began shortly thereafter. The structure, a dark abyss in the midst of the ice, foretold unsettling omens of death and madness. Arthur felt a shiver run down his spine. Eva, on the other hand, moved forward with an almost unnatural confidence, as if she had been there before.

The light outside slowly faded as they descended. The reddish light that reigned within enveloped them, and with it came a distant sound, a murmur that could not have come from any of the missing people. Arthur wanted to ask, wanted to stop, but Eva simply smiled at him.

"We're close," she whispered, and in the gloom, her eyes shone like frozen stars.

They advanced until they reached the fork in the tunnel. The light from their flashlights cast distorted shadows on the irregular walls. Eva paused briefly, then pointed to the left corridor without hesitation.

"This way," she commanded, her voice soft but firm.

Arthur followed her, feeling his legs weaken at the thought of peering into an abyss too deep for him. An abyss in which a darkness that was more than the mere absence of light wrapped around him like an irrevocable shroud.

Finally, the corridor opened into the vast pyramidal chamber, at the center of which stood the red-black trapezohedron. At the sides of the pyramid, seemingly contained by those almost imperceptible walls, unmoving, stood the beings shaped like twisted trees.

"Incredible..." Arthur murmured, unable to look away from those beings. "How long must those creatures have been trapped here?"

Eva, however, smiled with barely perceptible satisfaction. She knew exactly what she was seeing. "Their Firstborn," she whispered in awe, "the first of their lineage on Earth..."

"How long must those creatures have been trapped here?"

"Longer than you can imagine. But they're not trapped, Arthur, they were simply waiting for me."

"Waiting for you?"

"Wouldn't you wait millennia for me, Arthur?"

"Uh? Of course, my lady. Of course I would."

At that moment, Arthur, bewildered, watched as Eva, raising her hands to the sky, seemed to enter some kind of trance, while he could only stand there like a statue or, rather, like a puppet in need of a puppeteer to move it.

Eva, for her part, projected her astral body[3] from her physical form, attempting to communicate with the beings that inhabited the place. She knew how to do it; she had done so on numerous occasions with the younger siblings of those beings. It didn't take long for her to establish a relatively fluent communication with them, which she used to introduce herself as the high priestess of the cult that worshiped their mother, Shub-Niggurath. They quickly recognized her as such. Eva then stripped naked in front of an incredulous and astonished Arthur.

"Leave the equipment on the ground, Arthur. Come with me. I want to confirm something for myself, and I need your cooperation."

"Ye... Yes."

Together, they passed through one of the semi-transparent walls and approached one of those creatures. Arthur was terrified and wet himself when Eva ordered him to come closer to one of the beings, and he realized that, no matter how scared he was, he couldn't help but obey. He didn't even scream when the creature began to move and wrapped him in one of those tentacles that somehow resembled twisted branches. His fate was sealed, and his life had been useful to Eva. It had been worth living... Meanwhile, she licked her lips, gleefully watching the creature devour the poor wretch.

Then Eva approached the being and, confident in herself, gently placed one of her cold, soft hands on its "bark." Shortly thereafter, the creature possessed her, and she received it with great pleasure and devotion.

---

[3] The astral body is a subtle body believed to exist between the physical body and the soul. It is composed of astral matter, which vibrates at a higher frequency than physical matter.

Characteristics:
- It is an almost exact duplicate of the physical body.
- It is believed to be able to separate from the physical body and survive death.

Chapter 10
Flashes in the Darkness

In the distance, at the end of the long and silent tunnel they were in, they saw intermittent flashes of light, as if something were glowing with a life of its own in the midst of the darkness. Diop, driven by a mixture of anticipated relief and probably excessive enthusiasm, started running without a word, leaving his companions behind. In his mind, those flashes could well signal an exit to the open sky after hours of confinement underground.

It was something about that running that made Harun inexplicably recall how, as Diop, he had run just the way he was at that very moment, trying to reach some kind of mechanism on whose activation depended the lives of several thousand people living on a space station whose name he couldn't remember. It all played out in Harun's mind as a vague, foreign memory; however, he had no doubt that Diop's heroics had succeeded. On the other hand, that memory only amplified the image of cowardice Harun secretly had of himself. Ashamed, he said nothing and simply watched his Captain.

Upon reaching the end of the tunnel, what Diop found was not an exit but an irregular wall covered in hundreds of tiny crystals that seemed to sprout from the porous rock as if they were some kind of mineral excrescence. The lights he had seen were merely reflections, illusions multiplied by the perfectly polished surfaces of these formations. The Captain stopped dead in his tracks, panting, and barely had time to register the disappointment before something struck him with the subtlety of the impossible.

As soon as his reflection appeared in one of the crystals, he felt a dull throbbing in the center of his skull, something he could only describe as a heartbeat of emptiness sucking his mind dry. His thoughts dissolved like dust floating in the darkness. A second later, a strange lightness invaded his consciousness: it wasn't relief but something more like a loss of gravity, as if his mind no longer had any weight or anchor to reality.

He closed his eyes. The gasp that escaped him was almost a sob; something was wrong, terribly wrong, and although he was still conscious, he was no longer sure he was alone inside his head.

"Captain?" asked Kolab, who had followed close behind, noticing his reaction.

Diop shook his head, trying to dispel the mental fog. The image of his father... There was something about him that slipped away; he couldn't remember his face, couldn't remember his voice. The gap in his memory was palpable and drew his attention with unusual intensity, as if part of his identity had vanished. A chill ran down his spine and he felt his sanity teeter on an abyss as vertigo took hold of him.

"I saw myself reflected in those crystals... with my father. But... he vanished. From the crystal and from my mind, I no longer remember him, I don't know who my father was... I saw him, I know I did, but now he's gone, gone forever."

Harun, almost by reflex, couldn't help but look into one of the crystals. He didn't want to, but something stronger than his will compelled him; everything happened just as Diop had described, but the effect wasn't the same: Harun saw himself arriving on Pluto, with his companions, aboard the *Persephone*... and suddenly, his reflection disappeared. He forgot.

Anguish consumed him instantly. He blinked repeatedly, trying to find his bearings. The tunnel, the crystals, the elongated shadows cast by his companions... None of it made sense. He didn't know where he was, he didn't know what he was doing there. A feeling of unreality invaded him, and his fragile mind fractured into a thousand irreconcilable pieces.

"Where am I?! Who the hell are you people?!" he shouted, his face twisted in bewilderment, reflecting the utter terror he was experiencing.

Kolab reacted immediately.

"Cover your eyes! Don't look at the crystals!"

Everyone obeyed, except Harun, who collapsed to the ground in tears.

"We have to get through this corridor without looking at them. Something happened to Harun and to Captain Diop, and it seems it has to do with those things."

Aukan advanced cautiously, each step measured as if the floor might collapse beneath his feet at any moment, when suddenly he tripped on something, a bump in the terrain, a loose stone, or perhaps nothing at all, and in the impulse to avoid falling, he looked up and opened his eyes.

In front of him, nearly at face level, a small crystal jutted out of the wall. It had no defined shape, but one of its facets was polished enough to work like a mirror. Aukan froze. For one eternal instant, his reflection stared back at him with supernatural intensity, as if it weren't just a reflection, but something that thought for itself. Then confusion hit him like a brutal wave, dragging him out to sea.

Who was he?

He had just seen himself in the crystal: his eyes, his skin, the expression of astonishment. But behind the face, something else was revealed. Memories began to flow like an uncontrolled torrent: his childhood under the warm sunlight, playing in the mud, his parents' voices, the first time he ran without looking back. His teenage years, his youth... All of it appeared in flashes superimposed on his reflected face—and then everything vanished.

The memories disintegrated like ashes in the wind, dissolved with chilling ease, as if they had never belonged to anyone.

Aukan blinked, confused, trying to shake off the intense sensation of disorientation. He no longer remembered his childhood, nor his adolescence, nor his early youth. He didn't know who he was, he had no roots. What once was a human being now floated in an abyss without a history. The only thing left to him was the face in the crystal, a nameless echo and a growing sensation that someone or something was unmaking him from within.

The crystals seemed to observe them, patiently waiting for another fool to fall into their deception.

The end of the corridor was still far off, and with every meter traveled, the threat of being lost to oblivion became more real.

Harun's screams, now more distant, still echoed through the galleries: desperate echoes of the fate awaiting those unworthy of walking the labyrinth. No one looked back. No one said his name.

They had all lost something in that tunnel, some more than others, but no one came out unscathed.

"We can't go on like this," Diop said. "This... this is too much, it's destroying us. Who knows what other horrors lie beyond the next corner?"

"Where do I come from?" asked Aukan, his voice trembling. "I've forgotten where I was born. How is that possible? Fuck, how the hell is that even possible? Who the fuck am I?!"

"I don't know, Aukan. I don't know..." Kolab replied, listless, in a tone that suggested she was on the verge of giving up. "What is this place, Isabel?" she added.

Isabel, confused, looked at her. She opened her mouth but couldn't articulate a clear response.

"Where's that confidence in yourself now?" Diop snapped, with a mixture of anger and frustration.

Isabel swallowed hard. Several seconds passed as she tried to organize her thoughts, but she was unable to look any of them in the eye.

"This place... well, I don't know exactly," she began, hesitant, "but from what we could gather, countless eons ago it was a temple to which beings from different parts of the galaxy made pilgrimages."

"I can't grasp it..." Kolab murmured, dejected. "How have you been able to keep all this a secret? It's astonishing. How the fuck can you know all that? Fuck!"

"Damn witch..." Aukan muttered to himself.

"You don't understand anything," Isabel said with a glint of fanaticism in her eyes. "Our sacrifice is necessary. We cannot renounce knowledge. It's crucial."

"Nothing you're saying makes the slightest bit of sense," Diop replied with a trace of resignation. "Your words are mere distractions. I know you're lying to us."

"Then tell me, Captain... If there's no truth in my words, how is it we knew of the existence of this place?"

"And who cares about that now?" Diop snapped, exasperated.

"Well, for starters, those who pay you, Captain..."

Diop let out a bitter laugh.

"What does that matter now? We're not getting out of here..."

"We're not all getting out of here," Isabel corrected, with calculated coldness. "But I guarantee you, Captain, I have no intention of perishing in this labyrinth," Isabel said, now a little more sure of herself, raising her gaze again.

"Oh, really? And how do you plan to pull that off, little witch?" Aukan said with irony.

"To begin with, Aukan, by not showing desperation and cowardice to the lady of this place," Isabel replied, looking at him with disdain. "It seems clear that the first to fall wasn't exactly the bravest…"

Aukan fell silent. The truth was undeniable: Harun had been the first to succumb, and the most cowardly among them.

"I admit it won't be easy…" Isabel continued, with a nearly mystical smile. "My goddess is demanding, but we cannot allow those crystals to outshine our courage; it is the black flame of Shub-Niggurath that must guide us through the dark night of the soul."

Chapter 11
A New Hope

"We did it, Father, after so long the human species will finally take that evolutionary leap we so desperately needed."
—"Yes... finally. Still, I must admit I'm a little worried."
"And why is that?"
"We've put everything on this card and there are too many unknowns in the equation. Things that escape us."
"Big surprise, things always escape humanity," she laughed.
"Yes, I understand what you're saying, but..."
"But nothing, the priestesses are ready. They've dedicated their entire lives to this and we're not going to fail. Not us."
"I want you to lead the operation personally. I'm too old and my purpose has been fulfilled beyond my expectations."
"It looks like my moment has come, after this success no one will dare to question us."
"You're right, we've silenced many mouths."
"We don't know what they'll be like..."
"No, we don't."

"I've thought a lot about it..."

"Me too. There are too many possible scenarios..."

"If the litter born from the Firstborn retains their genetic purity, their development should enhance that capacity."

"Do you think the containment measures will be enough or should we reinforce them? We could unleash the greatest tragedy upon Earth, the end of the world."

"That won't happen. We didn't come this far just to screw it all up like that. And yes, it's true, if everything is as calculated, the power of the Firstborn, given their age, should be several times greater than that of their younger siblings."

"Sometimes I wonder who made it this far... and why."

"It's simple. We've reached the gates of apotheosis because we've desired it. It's that simple."

Chapter 12
The Astronaut

"There's no way out," Diop thought. "We're doomed to perish in this place that seems to exist beyond space-time. How is it possible that something like this exists? We think we're so grand, looking at the world through our pathetic arrogance."

"Captain, are you all right?" Kolab asked after noticing the worry appearing on his face.

He looked at her without answering, and suddenly, as if he had just remembered he could speak, he replied:

"Yes, it's just..."

"It's just that he's afraid," added Isabel, not without a hint of mockery, swaying like a pendulum between cautious insecurity and absurd arrogance.

Diop instantly recognized in Isabel that arrogance he had just been thinking about, and remained silent.

"What was that?" interrupted an unsure Aukan. "I saw something move at the end of the hallway."

"Yes, I thought I saw it too," Kolab confirmed.

"Hey!" Diop shouted just before starting to move toward the spot with considerable caution.

The others waited, alert, as their Captain faded into the purplish watery light that flooded the inhospitable place.

"Nothing," he was heard saying from the end of the hallway. Then the others caught up to him and confirmed his words.

"And yet, I'm sure there was something moving here."

"Yes, I saw it too. Damn it, this place is horrible. Sometimes I feel like I'm not entirely myself, I don't know if what I saw I saw with my own eyes or with yours... Fuck! Isn't there anything here I can beat the shit out of?" Aukan said, raising his voice.

Isabel smiled openly. She despised Aukan as much as Diop: they were too simple. Still, there was something about Diop's courage that was admirable, even she could recognize it.

"Seems not, Aukan, seems not..."

Kolab, trying to assess Aukan, came to the conclusion that he would be the next to fall. He wasn't ready for this, and Pluto was devouring him, both because of the moment he was going through, which astrologers knew so well, and because it was obvious this wasn't a challenge a poor man like Aukan could face.

"Aukan," Kolab said, "have you heard of Pluto's opposition to the natal Pluto that we all go through when we're around your age?"

He looked at her incredulously.

"I think in your case this could be closely related to the situation we are experiencing."

"And what could I do?" he replied with a docility very uncharacteristic of him, clearly showing the grim moment he was going through.

"Well, Pluto, according to astrology, has a function, you know?"

"Oh yeah? And what function is that?" Aukan said, regaining some of his arrogance.

"To eliminate what's not essential in the human psyche, to allow the rebirth of a being closer to themselves, without bullshit eclipsing their essence."

Aukan, puzzled, looked at her without understanding and, after a few seconds, replied:

"I don't think I should be worrying about that crap right now, Kolab..."

Just as Kolab had supposed, subtly challenging Aukan with "weird stuff" had the effect of putting him on the defensive, and it worked quite well to stop him from thinking about "weird stuff" in turn. She smiled slightly.

"There it is again!" Diop shouted as he ran toward the spot.

"Damn it!" he exclaimed. "It vanished again."

"Fuuuuuuuuuuck!" roared Diop, fed up with being toyed with.

And suddenly, he realized something: he knew his name, Pietro Diop, was false, but he no longer remembered his real name. He tried with all his strength, but it was impossible. His identity was slowly dissolving in that place. He knew it and he could do nothing about it, except try to keep control of himself.

"Easy, Captain, easy, let's not lose our cool," Isabel said, amused, as if playing an extremely stimulating game for her. Isabel knew she couldn't let herself be carried away by fear. She believed she had to maintain her characteristic arrogant attitude and not let external events influence her, and that's exactly what she was doing. In the end, wasn't it all just a staged attempt to test them? He smiled again.

"Let's not lose our cool?" Diop thought to himself. "Let's not lose our cool!" he finally shouted, his laughter booming, his eyes bloodshot and bulging. "Damn witch," he thought, just before lunging at her with a right hook ready to slam into Isabel's face.

But Isabel was no mere fortuneteller, and after uttering a few incomprehensible words, she left Diop trapped in her gaze, motionless, unable to do anything but wish for the nightmare to end once and for all.

"Captain," Isabel said with feigned patience, "I cannot allow you to use violence against me. You must understand that..."

Diop couldn't utter a word, and his head began to throb with intense pain at the temples.

"If you calm down, I could release you and make that annoying headache stop. On the other hand, if you don't, I'll kill you. Do you understand, Captain?"

Suddenly, Aukan jumped in alarm and pointed toward the place they had come from.

This time all of them, including Diop, who though petrified, maintained some control over his eyes, clearly saw what had been catching their attention: an astronaut was floating toward them, his feet not touching the ground, and his hand extended as if he wanted to reach them.

None could say which pair of eyes saw it first, because they all saw it as if they were one. And what they saw was, without a doubt, the most terrifying thing they had ever witnessed. It wasn't just an image; it was an omen. An omen of their own fate.

The helmet floated toward them, as if containing a scream trapped in the void. Inside was Harun, his face frozen in a rictus of agony. Dead, but still screaming: cold, blue, and pleading for a help that would never come.

Then, without warning, the image vanished. The astronaut disappeared before them, but he left something behind: the grim certainty that this would be the fate that awaited them all.

Chapter 13
A long-awaited journey

Mary took a deep breath, lost in thought, as the helicopter that would fly her to the archaeological site took off from a helipad about 40 km from the location.

She was nervous. Anyone who knew her could have noticed that... unconsciously she tried to adjust herself in her seat as if none of the slightly different positions she assumed were optimal enough to bring the peace her effervescent and troubled mind needed.

"It's so... how can I put it, I can't find the words, I've spent so many years fantasizing about this day..."

Mary looked out the window of the aircraft, as if searching for something that might give her some self-confidence, which, obviously, she didn't find. Not even the two built-in wardrobes that were her bodyguards could provide such a thing in a situation like that.

"Calm down, Mary, everything will be fine, humanity can no longer be what it has been until now, it's not acceptable, at least, not to humanity itself. It's time to move up a league, to go further than we've ever gone before. It's time to tear down the veil of ignorance that surrounds us, to knock down the walls of shame that imprison us like the zoo cages do to primates."

Outside the cabin, as if synchronizing with her besieged mind, a growing snowstorm was gaining importance, which in no way caused her any concern, being as she was immersed in her deepest thoughts and concerns.

"I wonder if Eva feels something similar, at least I don't have to fuck one of those things... Well, I'm sure Eva doesn't mind," she smiled. "She's never cared about those things. She's a pig."

The helicopter climbed a few hundred meters to clear the mountains surrounding the ancient site they were heading for. Fortunately for them, the onboard computer provided detailed terrain information since, to the naked eye, everything was just a vast white emptiness.

It's here, I can feel it, how it beats inside and outside of me, how it calls me from the distant past. Father, we are the chosen ones, we are the ones who will bring about the new world!

She felt like taking off the sunglasses that hid her milky, dead eyes; eyes she had sacrificed in pursuit of a clearer and deeper vision. She longed, more than ever before, to be able to see as she had during the early years of her life and thus behold the place.

"No, those things are irrelevant, damn it, I can't let my mind focus on such frivolities, fuck, what the hell is happening to me, this is important, Mary, it's the most important thing that has ever happened to humanity, damn it!"

"It's there! I'm going to start the descent," interrupted the pilot.

Mary, emitting a slight unclassifiable sound due to shock and confusion, "woke up" as if she had been immersed in a deep sleep for hours.

"Alright," she replied hesitantly while trying to regain her composure.

Then, she couldn't help but make a phone call to her father, she needed to hear his voice, get some advice, something, anything.

"Father?"

"Mary? Have you arrived already?"

"We're about to land..."

"Has something happened?"

"No, it's just that... well, I'm a bit nervous, the truth is I've spent so much time fantasizing and imagining what this day would be like, that now that finally, everything is happening as we wanted, well..."

"I understand, Mary, but you're strong, you've always been, this is your moment, your destiny, the goddess has chosen you, I know it very well."

"I need to know that you'll be by my side. I need that reassurance."

"Of course, of course I'll be by your side, you can count on my help and advice whenever you need it. I'm aware that the burden we must bear can be overwhelming at times, and it's obvious that this is one of those times, but you must be very clear about one thing, Mary: failure is not an option, focus on success, don't let fear or anxiety take over your attention, because that is the great enemy you'll face when making decisions of such importance."

"Thank you for your support, father, I'll call you later, after I've spoken with Eva and have a clearer idea of the situation."

"Goodbye, daughter, I know you'll succeed."

Mary hung up the phone and pretended to look out the window with her useless, dead eyes.

"My legs are shaking, that bitch will surely notice my nervousness the moment she sees me, damn it, I need to calm down, I can't act insecure, I'm convinced that, deep down, Eva thinks I'm not capable of carrying out such a task. I'm not my father."

The helicopter descended and softly landed on the blanket of freshly fallen snow that rested on its predecessors. Mary stepped out, displaying feigned self-confidence she did not feel, while Eva greeted her with a certain cordiality that was not at all usual in her, something that greatly surprised Mary.

"I thought your father would accompany you, Mary, but it seems you came alone. Well, not alone... your escorts are with you, but you know what I mean..."

"Yes, Eva, I understand. I thought your pregnancy wouldn't be... so obvious. After all, it's not even been a week."

"I thought so too, but you know, the power of those beings goes beyond anything we've ever known..."

"You were the first. Now there are already dozens of priestesses carrying their seed inside."

"We are willing to give everything for humanity. Our mission is crucial."

"Yes, we are all completely aligned with that."

"Come with me, Mary, it's very cold out here. Let's go inside the tent; there's hot coffee. Tell me, Mary, how is your father?"

"He's fine, but a trip like this... to such a remote place... It's not easy for someone his age."

Eva caressed her swollen belly while sipping hot coffee, already inside one of the tents.

"Mary, there's more here than just the Firstborns. As you know, the galleries the Mi-Go dug to extract that peculiar mineral are still here. But we've also found something else. An object of power. Something very... strange. We've never seen anything like it."

"What do you mean? You didn't report it."

"I know. I wasn't sure it was a good idea. I think it's influencing me somehow... Somehow, it advised me not to."

"This is absolutely irregular, Eva."

"Don't be so prissy, Mary, I already told you. The problem is... I'm drawn to it. It speaks to me in dreams."

"Oh, really? And what does it say?"

Eva remained tense in silence before answering.

"I don't know if I understand it well, but it seems someone is not happy with what we're doing. I must confess that... I feel some fear."

"But the goddess..."

"Yes, the goddess doesn't seem concerned. But I think the Mi-Go don't want to lose their position as her favorites, I don't know, it could be anything else... You know for the goddess, well, we can't really say she cares about us, or anything in this world. We're not capable of understanding her, you know that; the relationship with her is quite, how do I put it... numinous?"

"We knew that assuming a dominant role in the cosmic framework would generate tensions."

"Yes... but..."

"But what?"

"Do you think we are worthy?"

"What the hell are you saying, Eva?"

"I don't know... I think that thing is affecting me too much."

Mary leaned forward and lowered her voice.

"I'm in charge here. I order you and your priestesses to leave the site immediately. Our mission is too important to risk it because of your doubts. You must stay away from that object."

Eva lowered her gaze.

"There's something else..."

"What do you mean?"

"It's not the object that's communicating with me. I think the trapezohedron is just a transmitter, an instrument."

Mary's face hardened.

"Then who is speaking to you?"

Eva swallowed.

"I think it's one of their hives."

Mary's stomach clenched.

"Are you serious?"

"Yes. I think we've finally made contact with one of their great colonies... and they want us to abandon our project."

Mary narrowed her eyes.

"They'd better get used to it. There's a new player in the game now."

"They told me why they came to our system... There's something out there. An ancient place, older than them. A site where, at least in part, our goddess dwells."

"What? What do you mean?"

"They say we must stop our expansion into the cosmos. That under no circumstances should we go there... to that ancient citadel. And I think they're right, Mary. We shouldn't go..."

"I don't recognize you, Eva. I really don't recognize you."

Eva was trembling. For the first time in decades, she seemed... scared. She looked at her belly with an expression of horror, as if she had just awakened from a long dream, as if she finally understood the true nature of what she was carrying. Thick tears began to roll down her face.

Chapter 14
Not Being

"It was Parmenides of Elea who, more than two millennia ago, formulated the revolutionary maxim:"

'Being is, and non-being is not.'

"Perhaps it was true until yesterday. Or maybe it hasn't been for a long time. Or never was. Who can know?"

"Not even memory anymore, that last fragile witness of what once was, seems to remain."

"How can I know if I stopped existing some indeterminate time ago, and what speaks now, this that thinks, this that remembers, is nothing more than the lingering echo of something already extinguished?"

'You cannot bathe twice in the same river.'

"And I feel it with every fiber of my being. Nor can you remember the same memory twice…"

"Then, how is it possible that I still recognize myself?"

"Maybe I don't. Maybe I simply reflect myself, moment after moment, in a mirror that also flows, in which I appear only to disappear with a blink."

"Yes, that reflection cannot last more than a breath. And yet, I cling to it as if I could remain immutable there."

"I live in an eternal flow, a transit with neither source nor destination; I am not a being, but a sequence of flashes between two darknesses without identity. There are no eternal laws, no permanent matter; what is, fades away, what was, never repeats in the same way."

"And we, poor points of consciousness, fleeting passengers in the torrent... try to define ourselves, to fix ourselves, to be. But how do you define what never stops transforming?"

"Perhaps what we are is nothing more than the desperate attempt to remember... the desire to keep appearing in that mirror, even knowing that reflection is not eternal and not even the same reflection that was a second ago..."

"Kolab? Answer me, damn it!" said a desperate Diop, watching how every few minutes his crew sank a bit deeper into the unfathomable abyss of their own minds.

"Kolab... That's what you used to call me. Yet now I remember some of your most secret memories as my own... Doesn't that mean I'm no longer just Kolab, Captain Diop? Or would it be more accurate to say, Captain Pellegrini? Considering you've changed your name several times to hide your past, I wouldn't know what to call you..."

Diop took a step back upon hearing that name. It was evident that the name had once meant something to him, but he couldn't remember, couldn't identify it... Like all the other members of the crew, Diop was slowly dissolving like a sugar cube in a cup of hot coffee.

Aukan watched them in astonishment, terrified. He had no way to confront such emptiness that was gradually flooding their minds, leaving behind a trail of nothingness that filled with memories that weren't theirs. He screamed, with all his soul, with all his rage. The silence, mute witness to his despair, enveloped him.

Isabel watched them, her own mind fragmented in pieces, fully aware that some of those fragments came from her companions. She had undergone extremely harsh trials to enter the Order; at times she believed she wouldn't make it, yet she always pulled through. This time would be no different, she told herself, trying to summon the courage to believe her own words.

"Follow me," Diop finally said, drawing strength from weakness, and began to walk forward, dragging his feet in a superhuman effort.

The others, gathering what little strength they still had, followed him, partly grateful that someone was still pulling the cart at this point.

The progress seemed, at least from their perspective, painfully slow. Their tired vision, bathed in the liquefied violet light, seemed submerged at the bottom of a dead sea that was, little by little, dissolving their souls. And suddenly, without realizing anything other than the simple fact that they were still moving forward, they found themselves in a vast chamber.

A huge room, circular in shape. The boundaries of the space blurred, as if its walls were only suggestion, fragments of alien dimensions projected onto the fragile human mind. In its center, rising with a merciless solemnity that oppressed the soul, stood a motionless creature vaguely reminiscent of a dry tree, twisted beyond all naturalness.

A pestilent breath permeated the air. The surfaces vibrated with a muffled pulse, as if the floor were breathing. None recognized it for what it truly was.

None except Isabel.

She knew exactly what it was... That creature was none other than one of her goddess's children. She felt the black flame of Shub-Niggurath burning inside her. She knew her mere presence had awakened it. And she also knew there was no way to face it, no way to appease it. The time for resistance had passed, now all that remained was to run and pray to a deity that knew nothing of prayers.

"Run!" she screamed in desperation, that word torn from the depths of her being.

The creature opened its eyes. Not one or two, but many. And of them, as one,, fixed their focus on them. They didn't look at them: they pierced them. And with every second, with every stare, something inside each of them began to unravel. It was not bodies fleeing, but memories spilling out like ink in water, as if the very idea of "I" began to rot under the weight of that vision.

And then, the chamber ceased to be a chamber. Time ceased to be time.

And they, those who still believed they were, began to understand what it meant to not be.

Chapter 15
The Protocol

"Elder Brother, what should we do now? Perhaps we could begin deploying the protocol set to precede the revelation?"

"Not yet, Vargas, not yet. Too many things are hanging by a thread right now. We won't begin deployment until success is 100% guaranteed."

"I understand, it's just that, well, you know, so much time has passed…"

"I know. Humanity will know at the right moment; after all, all of this has been done for the common good."

"True, all for the people, but without the people… at least for now…"

"Exactly. Few have sacrificed as much as you have; don't you think we've forgotten that. Ordinary people have paid with their ignorance, but we too have paid a great price for this."

"You know I didn't do it for personal glory. Everything I've done, no matter how horrible it may seem, I've done it solely for humanity."

"When do you intend to give the order?"

"When the brood, already developed and in perfect harmony with the priestesses, can be presented to the public. I don't want anything to fail."

"Then there's still quite a way to go…"

"Yes, I understand your enthusiasm, but we can't risk even the slightest mistake. We can't reveal our hand, not even to ourselves, until everything is arranged with the utmost care."

"Of course. It shall be done that way."

"Yes, I know. We all know," Vargas said, taking his leave.

"I wonder how events will unfold. There are so many pieces that must fit together with absolute precision, and we know so little about them…"

"Human thought is light, ephemeral the consciousnesses that face those 'gods' who dwell beyond even the space that we can't truly call a place, since we are merely passing through it with barely any understanding of it."

"How could we possibly comprehend the dwelling of a god? And yet, we intend to wield their power for our own glory."

"The moment is so close now, with the safeguards of what once seemed impossible already fallen, that I am terrified. How will we be remembered? Will anyone remain to do so?"

"Most people are simply content to live their lives without asking too many questions… They're not concerned about the place of the human species in the cosmos, nor do they want to know anything about those who, long before them, long before us, inhabited the planet Earth. Who am I to wake them from their comfortable, stupid slumber? Do we have the right to do so?"

"If I didn't, if I were to back down now, what would have been the point all those crimes we've committed in pursuit of a greater end? Our end does justify the means, we often say…"

"I can't believe this. How can I be thinking these things right now, when it's already so late, when we're already so close…"

The Elder Brother, tense and trying to think of other things, left the control room with a succession of weary steps, heading toward his quarters, ready to rest.

That night, and despite the medications prescribed by some of the finest doctors, he found himself haunted by fiery nightmares in whose flames, like a dark alchemy, the faces of all those who had been sacrificed for the cause dissolved and coagulated in an endless game.

Chapter 16
Desperation

"I must run faster," Harun thought as he fled from that horrible creature that had just awakened, after who knows how many centuries or millennia of oblivion. He remembered himself in that damned house, trying to hide in the few hiding places it could offer and in the vain hope that his father would eventually forget about him.

"It's strange, thought Harun as he ran, I could swear Harun was left behind, I saw his body floating in the void, with that expression of horror drilled into his face…"

Harun stopped abruptly, dazed, looked at one of his hands and didn't recognize it: how could he have, if it was a woman's hand? Isabel found herself staring, amazed, at her own hand. She resumed running, driven by an increasingly intense fear.

Kolab looked around only to realize that, after her frantic run trying to escape the terrible emerging being, she had separated from the group and was now completely alone in that nightmarish place.

She screamed with as much desperation as futility. Trying to communicate with any of the crew members, she used the intercoms, which seemed not to work, cried in despair and, finally, resumed her aimless race.

After several minutes, exhausted, she collapsed onto the firm ground that held that madness.

"There's no way out. This place beat us from the damned beginning, and we're not capable of doing anything but prolonging the agony."

"Indeed," she thought with some irony, "this is a 'non-place'. Here, one is merely passing through and, of course, incapable of assigning any meaning to the space. Of course! How could a mere human assign meaning to the space where a goddess dwells? All of this is ridiculous… Isn't it obvious that there are no patterns here? That's something proper to small human minds: we need them to give things meaning… Why would a god need something like that?"

"The same laws do not apply here as they do in the human world, this isn't even the reality I've inhabited my whole life. Here, my world dies like a simple wave reaching a solid shore. This is neither benevolent nor malevolent; it's simply a boundary we should never have crossed."

Diop ran completely disoriented, looking around in search of his childhood, which had long been left behind. "Mom, where are you?" he shouted inside a mind that wasn't his own but Aukan's, who, in turn, was running without knowing who he was or where he was going.

Suddenly, someone crashed into someone. Kolab, partially aware of who she was, recognized Diop, though he, lost in a sea of foreign memories, was unable to react until she shouted at him for the umpteenth time, pronouncing his name preceded by the word "Captain."

"Where?"

"Captain, it's Kolab, do you recognize me?"

"Ko..."

"Kolab, Captain, we're in..."

"Pluto, we're on Pluto."

"Exactly, Captain, we're on Pluto."

Diop looked around and, seeing no one else, asked Kolab with his eyes.

"Do you remember that creature with dozens of eyes, Captain?"

The Captain had to think for several eternal seconds before fearfully nodding his head.

"Good... what happened is that we all ran and got separated during the escape."

"Damn it" exhaled a Diop more dead than alive.

"I don't know what to do, Captain... This is the dwelling of a god, and we should never have come here."

"I know, but we can't give up."

Those last words surprised Kolab, who thought she had lost all hope while trying, deep in her soul, to find a final spark of determination.

"Get up, Kolab. If we came in here, we can also get out of here."

It was amazing how Diop kept getting back on his feet no matter how hard the blows he took. Kolab began to understand why someone like him had been chosen to lead a mission like this...

They moved forward, wrapped in the characteristic purplish and watery glow that prevailed in the space they were wandering through. Kolab, once again, chose to rest one of her hands on the wall and not remove it in order to avoid getting lost.

As for Aukan, who was already more than just Aukan, as memories of his own and others danced in his mind, mingling together, diluting the essence of his being, he continued wandering through the tunnels, now completely lost and blaming himself for all the atrocities he had committed in his past, because, without a doubt, at least in what remained of his mind, he was in hell, paying for them all.

He begged forgiveness from all those he left behind and whom he had often mocked as weaklings who, at least, had been useful to him. That was, clearly, his greatest achievement.

He pleaded for the mercy of those who, uninvolved in his conflicts, had perished by his hand simply for being in the wrong place at the wrong time.

He even spoke to God. Aukan had to find himself in such a situation to address God a few words… Obviously, that god did not answer. However, rising from the deepest part of his being, a distant mocking laugh emerged.

Chapter 17
Silence

Mary took command of the excavation, eliminated all the unwelcome witnesses working on the site, and replaced them with personnel she completely trusted. She then descended into the alien subterranean for the first time to explore the site and get a first impression. She was accompanied by two armed men and a priestess named Déifila, who had not been impregnated by the Firstborn and whose mission was to try to establish some kind of communication with them or with whatever was transmitting from the cosmos through the trapezohedron.

Déifila, fascinated, marked the path forward with confidence while carefully observing everything that rose up around her. Mary, on the other hand, more cautious, followed her steps, unable to avoid being occasionally distracted by her thoughts.

"At last I will achieve the recognition I deserve within the organization. I'm tired of living in my father's shadow. Now it's my moment. Now they'll see what I'm capable of on my own."

Meanwhile, far away, somewhere in Eastern Europe, isolated in an ancient castle, her father, the Elder Brother Emeritus, paced in circles by the light of a fireplace, over an old wooden floor that creaked under his weight just as his mind creaked under the burden of the fate that was about to arrive, in a majestic chamber filled with ancient and comfortable furniture.

"She's too self-confident, she's just like her mother. The last thing that would ever cross her mind is that her own failure is an option. We have too much at stake, but I'm too old now and she's the only one I can pass the torch to…"

"I don't understand why she decided to send all the impregnated priestesses back to Europe. There's still a long time before they start giving birth. I get the impression she just wanted to get Eva out of the way. I can't really blame her for that."

Interrupting his train of thought, he stopped in front of a huge, exquisitely crafted oil portrait in which a 15th century aristocrat was depicted.

"So it all started with a text that someone in Castile translated from Arabic and, for some reason, ended up in your hands… Life, right?"

"Nah, we no longer believe in coincidences. It's impossible for us to consider such a thing feasible. We leave those little white lies to the people who like to say they live with their feet on the ground. Little ants, with all their little legs stuck firmly to the ground," he laughed.

The group reached the fork, and although they had originally planned to enter the mining area first, Mary couldn't resist heading straight toward the wing where the Firstborn were found, dwelling in those peculiar pyramids with almost transparent walls, along with the trapezohedron.

"I always knew my seed was sown by the gods, buried in the shadow of my father, waiting for the dawn. At last, at last it is my time; the glorious sun calls to me."

Upon arriving before the creatures, Déifila, utterly fascinated, knelt before them and began a series of reverential chants that demonstrated her complete submission. Ever since she was "rescued" from an orphanage by The Brotherhood, her life had been dedicated to serving them in every possible way. Having achieved such a level of responsibility for her people was not just a reward, it was her chance to repay her benefactors by giving one hundred percent of herself.

However, neither Mary nor Déifila were able to establish any form of communication with the Firstborn, who, along with the trapezohedron, remained in absolute silence.

Both they and several experts who were part of the mission tried, in various ways, to reestablish the communication that Eva and her acolytes had initially managed to create with the beings found there. However, all these efforts were in vain.

"We're missing something," Mary thought from her private quarters, reluctantly considering the possibility of contacting Eva and asking for her advice (something she found humiliating).

"How can they remain silent? After millennia of confinement, we've finally found them, it should be something positive for them. Or is it that they already have what they wanted?"

"We're going to use their power. From now on, they'll serve us, no matter how much they resist. They need to understand that it is now The Brotherhood who, under the protective umbrella of their Mother, gives the orders here."

The situation, to the despair of everyone and especially of Mary, remained stagnant for the following weeks. Driven by growing desperation, Mary ordered mediums and sorcerers to be brought from different parts of Earth, as well as a large number of priestesses. None of whom were able to communicate with the Firstborn. In the end, given the overwhelming frustration, it was decided to build a dome over the ruins to function both as a scientific facility and a sarcophagus, within which the Firstborn would remain sealed. The objective was clear: keep the site under control while waiting for breakthroughs that would allow the research teams to resolve the situation.

Mary, for her part, abandoned the site and returned, deeply frustrated, to the facilities where her father usually resided.

Chapter 18
The Thousand Faces of the Minotaur

Isabel advanced alone and lost, searching for the help of an Ariadne who had never existed, at least not for her. She knew she was being stalked by that creature with a thousand eyes, by that son of her goddess who would not stop until he had finished them all.

How was that possible? Hadn't she devoted her life to serving her lady with absolute devotion?

"Of course," she smiled, "like so many others I saw succumb, like so many others who served with devotion and whom I always considered unworthy, using those assumptions to elevate myself, in my delusion, above them all and believing that my destiny was different, much higher, just like my own nature. How stupid I was..."

Isabel, shedding tears in a humble silence, walked on, uncertain, fearing that around every corner the creature with dozens of eyes could be waiting—a creature who was, by all appearances, the guardian of the place.

"How different I am from Theseus. I have no one's help in this place, and it's become painfully clear that I'm no mythological heroine. Obviously, this time it won't be the Minotaur who ends up dead. I feel like he's waiting confidently in the center of the labyrinth, ready to finish us off and with the logical certainty that he doesn't need to bother chasing us."

"Here I am, monster, end this farce once and for all!"

Kolab thought he heard a scream coming from somewhere indeterminate within the labyrinth. She could have sworn it was Isabel's voice, but she had no way of pinpointing its origin, let alone heading toward it.

"Did you hear that, Captain?"

"Yes, though I couldn't locate the source…"

"I think it was Isabel."

"That damn witch, she knew all along where we were going…"

"I'm not so sure about that. It's clear she knew something, but I think right now she's just as trapped and overwhelmed as any of us…"

"Poor thing…" Diop added sarcastically.

"We've been walking for so long, and except from a few specific places, everything looks the same here. It's possible there are still more of those unique chambers we can find. This labyrinth doesn't seem to have a defined structure, and things don't appear to be located in just one place…"

"You're right about that, Kolab."

"Do you think there could be some way to make it easier to find those unique places?"

"I wouldn't know how to do something like that… All I can do is keep moving forward, Aukan."

"I understand, Captain, but I'm Kolab…"

"Right…"

"Everything is so confusing here. Sometimes I remember Harun's childhood more clearly than my own, if I'm not confusing it with one of yours... I try not to think about it."

"I think the only thing maintaining any kind of internal cohesion in my mind right now is the desire to escape. I don't remember my father, Kolab. I don't know who he was..." Diop said, bursting into tears.

"Captain, I need you to stay strong. We can't sink into the mental sea of confusion this place throws us into."

"It's like what Isabel said, about the 'non-places'. We're just passing through here, since this space has nothing to offer us, right? It seems like something similar is happening with our identities, as if a human identity could simply be a place of passage, without real meaning."

"I understand what you're saying, Captain, and I admit it makes a lot of sense. We're facing something completely new for humanity, though we always have the option to give our own meaning to the space we inhabit, as well as to our own mind or identity. Many claim there's no real difference between the exterior and the interior. I think this place could symbolize the union between a god and humanity. I think that might be its meaning, or at least between a god and the different species that might one day reach the place."

"And what good does that do us?"

"I believe the more we know about the place, the more we'll know about how to get out..."

"The more I know about this place, the less I know about myself. I'm fragmenting, I'm blending with all of you..."

"I'm also losing many memories, and I'm being invaded by others that aren't mine... I try to focus on getting out of here. It terrifies me to think about it..."

"Are you sure I'm the Captain of this mission? You keep repeating it, but I have to confess I don't remember leading this mission."

"I'm sure."

"And what if our identities were like shadows dissolving under the light the divine casts upon us, revealing the illusion of existence for what it's always been: a simple farce?"

"Captain, as the onboard therapist, I strongly recommend you put those thoughts aside and focus on getting out of here. I need you, Captain. I need you leading all of this."

For her part, Isabel, wandering the hallways and trying to determine whether her real name was Aukan, Isabel, or something else entirely, wondered how much that even mattered.

"They could be two, two thousand, or all the souls that have been, are, and will be... orbiting around me, merging into a single will. Why not? Isn't that what pulses beneath the skin of the universe? A Leviathan, yes, like Hobbes's, but self-aware, awakened... and me at its core: the all-seeing eye, the center where the lines of time and flesh converge."

"Of course! That is the next evolutionary step. I understand now, Mother. Everything will revolve around me. I will be the center around which the new human colossus will orbit."

"That is the gift my goddess has reserved for humanity. And this place... this place is the threshold someone had to cross to earn the blessing."

"I must find the others and share the good news, tell them of their privileged and central role in what is to come. I finally understand, Mother, finally..."

Chapter 19
The Birth

Eva and her acolytes, who had obeyed Mary in everything she ordered, traveled to an ancient prehistoric "temple" erected in caves deep within the Carpathians Mountains countless millennia ago by an unknown humanity. The place was nothing more than a series of galleries and caverns whose walls featured a series of cave paintings depicting the goddess and a crude stone sacrificial altar. To make it habitable, it had been remodeled adding several annexes, including living quarters for the priestesses who there, in the depths, worshipped their usually indifferent goddess. It was also in that place where all of them, in the coming days, would give birth to the dark offspring they carried in their corrupted wombs.

All the priestesses, without exception, were familiar with the place, yet that did not stop them from feeling overwhelmed during the descent into the facility. Perhaps it was the smell of dampness on the ancient stone, combined with the twisted shapes in which the rock seemed to have formed, creating that hidden world where someone, long ago, had chosen to paint those cave motifs. Or perhaps it was something else, something emanating from the beyond.

Everything was in place: a group of priestesses who had not been impregnated by the Firstborn, along with a team of doctors of the highest caliber in medicine, pharmacology, biology, and so on, were "ready" to take care of everything.

Everyone in the facility knew the outcome was imminent, and that was why some of the pregnant priestesses began to feel the kind of fear that fanatics are incapable of feeling until they begin to open their eyes.

The scene was impressive: the priestesses, naked and surrounded by the crying of several babies waiting to be delivered to the Great Mother, walked along the galleries and gradually congregated in the central cavern, in front of the sacrificial altar, which could only be vaguely perceived carved into the rock.

Eva officiated the ceremony, chanting a series of guttural songs while, to the greater glory of her goddess and as a sign of devotion, she slit the throats of the newborns one by one.

The ceremony lasted several hours, during which the priestesses, in their completely altered states of consciousness, tried with varying degrees of success to prepare their bodies and minds for what awaited them...

Only two days passed after the ceremony before everything unraveled.

"I'm so afraid," Eva thought. "I know I'm going to die. The creature inside me speaks to me in my dreams. It doesn't recognize me as its mother; its mother is Shub-Niggurath... I am merely a vessel, and it has assured me that, as such, I will be discarded when my function is fulfilled. I wish I could destroy it, but no one here will help me, and I am powerless to do anything. I don't want to die, not by my own hand..."

"There I was, so young, I don't remember exactly when, but back then, I was truly young. I remember how fascinated I was to be part of something dark and elitist like the cult of Shub-Niggurath. I felt so good, so powerful... I can't deny that feeling lasted for decades, until very recently."

Eva remembered herself walking, almost gliding across the floor like a dry leaf trying to fly by itself without ever touching the ground. Her mentor awaited her at the end of the tunnel carved into stone, at the inner end of which was the chamber where she would officially be named a priestess. She had never felt anything like it. It wasn't just an intense sense of personal validation: it was something more, something ecstatic, something not of this world.

She did what she had to do: she took the life of that baby. How many had it been already? Impossible to remember, she told herself...

She left there so sure of herself... Walking firmly, with her chin raised, radiating that determination and power that would allow her not only to stand out in the Order, but to rise above all her peers as their high priestess.

"How did I end up here? I thought I was doing something important, something good, or so I told myself... It was all out of vanity. I never cared about anyone beyond myself, no matter how many times I told myself that someone exceptional like me should serve humanity and that that's what I was doing. It was all lies. In the end, I was just a foolish, vain woman, and these tears running down my face are my only reward."

She thought about all this while looking in the mirror at her haggard face, which was now nothing more than a distorted, caricature-like reflection of the beautiful face she had once had. It was then that the first terrible contractions began.

Terrified, she immediately alerted the medical team and was rushed to one of the operating rooms. To her misfortune, it had been decided that births should be carried out without anesthesia, to avoid any effects on the offspring.

"Please, Mother, I always served you with devotion. Despite your indifference, I was always there, doing what you wished... Or was it us who wished it?"

That last thought crossed her mind, not for the first time, although she always dismissed it. She so desperately wanted to believe that her goddess was aligned with their practices that she avoided acknowledging the goddess's manifest indifference as a sign of anything else.

"No, I can't falter now. It's too late. This was my wager, and I have to accept it to the very end. Isn't Shub-Niggurath powerful enough to ensure this all ends well? I am her most devoted servant. She will never discard me. Everything will be fine, I know it, mother, I know it… AAAAAARGH!"

The pain was unbearable. Her belly swelled and deflated arrhythmically as she screamed in abominable agony.

"Pain purifies me, mother, and it is through it that I come closer to you, with devotion and… AAAAAAAAAARGH!"

Suddenly, as her ribs cracked and broke, everything went black for her. In the operating room, it was her ruptured guts that stained the sterile white walls red—the same walls where symbols had been engraved to facilitate the births. That white, like the pale skin of Eva, whose icy eyes cried as they melted into the immensity of the void.

At first, the horrifying darkness that burst from Eva's shattered body watched for a few seconds with its multiple red eyes at the stunned staff in the room. One of the doctors couldn't bear the horror, despite being fully aware of what was going to happen and having seen more than a few ultrasounds of the being, and collapsed unconscious on the floor.

It was at that moment, "taking advantage" of the confusion, that the creature lunged at the unfortunate wretch who had just fainted.

While all this was happening, the priestess present in the room tried in vain to communicate with the creature, but, at least at first glance, it didn't seem to be happening.

No one attempted to separate the creature from its victim, who was completely devoured within minutes.

For some reason, no one tried to flee the room. Perhaps they all believed that if they didn't pass out, they were safe. Who knows...

The priestess was the second to be attacked by one of the twisted, spiky tentacles. It was then that the rest of the team finally reacted. They all tried to escape, but those who, from their distant and safe offices, watched everything that was happening, prevented the operating room door from opening, condemning them all to die there.

After the disaster, many of the priestesses and doctors tried to flee. However, to their despair, the facility was sealed from the outside.

The hybrid offspring took control of the site and entered some form of hibernation which, after feeding on the humans they found there, would allow them to develop into their adult forms.

Several days passed before a special Brotherhood team was sent to inspect the underground facility. It consisted of five men and two women, all veterans of the organization, experts in anomaly containment and evidence collection. They descended wearing biological protection suits and autonomous recording equipment, escorted by combat drones.

What they found down there left an indelible mark on their memories. The galleries were covered in a viscous, black substance that seemed to faintly throb with a life of its own. In the operating rooms, the few remains of the medical team that could still be found lay torn apart, their faces frozen in expressions of absolute terror.

One of The Brotherhood members, Brother Kárász, found a bloodstained notebook in one of the rooms. It belonged to Eva. Inside was a delirious collection of prayers and poems dedicated to her Mother.

Meanwhile, the creatures remained motionless, in a latent state that seemed to only allow them to grow and develop their bodies slowly.

They took samples, photographs, everything they could... and then, with trembling hands, activated the sealing protocol. The temple doors were closed with ritualized steel plates and buried under tons of reinforced concrete. A sanctuary turned tomb.

None of the recordings were distributed beyond the inner circle of the cult's leadership. Upon reading the report, Mary knew her era had ended. The images of Eva screaming in madness, the creatures rising from pools of viscera, and the general disaster... were more than the organization could tolerate.

Mary received the report in her sanctum, an ancient library filled with shelves of some especially dark oak that served as her office. She read it in complete silence. With every page she turned, her knuckles grew whiter, until finally she let the dossier fall onto the desk with an almost human gesture of exhaustion. She could no longer deny the obvious: she had failed.

The vision of Eva destroyed, the audiovisual records leaked from the operating room, screams still echoing inside the sterile metal, and the remains of the blood-soaked temple took from her the last of her faith. Not faith in the goddess, for Shub-Niggurath remained, immutable, but in herself. She had believed she could master chaos. She had believed, with the arrogance of emperors, that she could guide the will of an entity that knew nothing of human concepts like greed or loyalty.

The "resignation" was neither public nor honorable. It was written in an encrypted message, sent only to the upper circle. "I am no longer worthy of interpreting the Mother's will," it said, "and perhaps I never was. Let another one continue this path, if there is still a path left to follow."

No one cared what happened to her anymore. The only certainty was that her disappearance left a void. And where there is void, struggle is born. The following decades were marked by bloody schisms and internal purges. Many left the organization, as if the goddess herself watched the collapse of her cult with the same indifference with which she watches the sprouting of a spore or the death of a star.

After the long period of internecine warfare to gain control of the cult, a new Elder Brother was able, with the help of new technologies, to "triangulate" the origin of the communications Eva had received from the trapezohedron found in the Arctic excavations. From that it was possible to locate the exact point to which, later on, the *Persephone* had been sent.

Chapter 20
The Oracle

What Aukan had become saw them from afar, undetected by any of them, whatever their names were at this point. "Aukan" knew a lot about them, knew their deepest fears, because he was also, in part, them as well.

As he watched them, he savored how the one who had once been his Captain had enjoyed, like him, taking lives just for money, just to fulfill a mission in which a stranger ordered him to kill another stranger.

"A no-place, a no-ego, that's what eternity is," he thought, free from castrating identities, from illusory purposes that only serve to keep alive the illusion of separation between one and another.

He laughed inside; now he was capable of grasping concepts that had always been beyond his short understanding. Now he knew of ontologies and epistemologies, of phenomena and noumena…

"That damned Diop, giving orders as if he were above the rest… I will absorb him, devour his soul as I consume his flesh and take all his power. That's how things work here," he growled.

"I know that in ancient times some warriors would devour the hearts of fallen enemies to absorb their powers. That's how things work," he laughed madly.

With wild, bloodshot eyes, Aukan crept forward only to realize that, while he was thinking about what he was going to do, he had lost sight of both Diop and Kolab.

"It's so strange, Kolab, I feel no physical fatigue and yet, my mind can't go on. I can't stand to turn another corner and see, on the other side, the same thing we left behind."

"I understand you, Captain. I feel like I'm losing my mind. On the one hand, as I already told you, I think we should get to know this place better so we can assess it more accurately and find the way out. But on the other hand, I can't bear getting lost in theoretical philosophical considerations about the labyrinth. I'm sorry if I was harsh with you earlier when I told you to stop your thoughts. I'm having trouble maintaining acceptable levels of coherence... I should be able to handle this situation, I'm the psychoanalyst on board, it's my responsibility to maintain some level of sanity."

"Don't worry, Kolab, don't worry about that now..."

Kolab approached the Captain. She was crumbling inside and at that moment, she just needed someone to hold her.

He, still disoriented, hugged her awkwardly at first, but soon they clung to each other like shipwrecked souls grabbing a wooden plank floating in the vast sea. The kiss came without words, intense and urgent, like a mythical balm poured over hearts already on the brink of ruin.

What followed was an act of surrender as deep as it was strange: their bodies united in a communion that transcended the physical, the individual.

They were not alone.

Throughout the act, the minds of the rest of the *Persephone's* crew, sleeping, present, absent or dead, vibrated in tune with theirs. A multiple presence, invisible but undeniable, arose from the depths of their souls. As if they all shared that intimacy.

Aukan, who had heard their moans, approached them with extreme care, as a black panther would do under a black sky in pursuit of prey. However, he was not alone. Something had followed him there, something enormous with as many eyes as those that peer into those black nights where he grew accustomed to hiding so many unspeakable secrets.

It all happened quickly: suddenly, Aukan, who was about to pounce on Kolab and Diop, was lifted into the air by a mass of writhing tentacles emerging from that abject dark body, in which a myriad of eyes shone as red as the blood they longed to shed.

Kolab and Diop ran, never looking back. There was no need: the screams of Aukan were more than enough for them to understand what was happening behind.

They fled the place without direction until they couldn't go on, driven by the most intense horror imaginable. Finally, exhausted, they collapsed beside each other.

They tried to speak but simply couldn't... How could they? How to explain in words what they had felt during that sexual act in which they hadn't been alone? How to speak of the mental fragments of their companions who, though dead, still lived within them?

Isabel, meanwhile, continued to wander the place, convinced that she had to find her companions and explain what was happening. Wasn't she the axis of the wheel around which all humanity would revolve, thus transcending into a new and superior evolutionary stage?

"Kolab, where are you? We have to talk, it's very important that you understand... I already have, and it's wonderful. We are lucky to have come this far, it was our destiny to be the first ones!"

"How could I have been so afraid? I laugh just thinking about it now; it's all so obvious... Oh, Shub-Niggurath, I, your most devoted servant, have been chosen by you to bear upon my shoulders this evolutionary leap by which all humanity will transcend into new and fascinating realities that dwell beyond the veils of Isis. I, Isabel."

"Captain, listen to me, there's no reason to worry anymore, I swear, I understand now. Don't hide. I need to speak with you and the others! You must merge with me before we can leave this place, so we can assimilate the rest of humanity around us. We are all one, Diop, we are all one!"

While Isabel wandered, deliriously through the corridors in search of her companions, Kolab began to recover from the shock she had suffered and, together with Diop, tried to get up.

Diop looked at her in silence, as if trying to convey something far beyond language.

They helped each other to stand up and, in silence, they continued their erratic wandering through the walls of the mute labyrinth.

It was no longer hope that guided their steps, it was something else, something more similar to some kind of inertia that, somehow, knew that under no circumstances could it stop if it wanted to continue existing.

Countless hours passed as they silently kept walking, chasing a miracle that might save not just their bodies, but their souls. All the while, their increasingly confused minds were gradually forgetting their individual identities, assimilating memories slipping into their imaginations like a virus into a healthy organism.

"We are alone, Captain. There's no one else left here..."

"We know nothing about Diop."

"You are Diop, Captain..."

"What? Oh yes, of course... I meant Isabel."

"I know, but I'm convinced that there is little left of what she once was... That's if the monstrous creature we found hasn't already done to her what it did to Aukan. In that case, there might be nothing left of her at all."

"True, we must... must go on, Isabel..."

Kolab looked at him, saying nothing. It was evident that Diop was increasingly struggling to use the correct names. Still, she admired his determination to keep going despite everything.

"We won't get out of here, I'm sure of it. Diop won't last much longer, and I won't either, not without him. This place and what it can do is, in every way, far beyond any category the human mind can even begin to comprehend."

"How could I communicate to the outside world what's happening here? At least then it would make sense that we came this far... Now, looking back, I feel that my life wasn't what I wanted it to be. Now that I am also Harun, Isabel, Aukan, and Diop, I have access to many other perceptions, emotions, thoughts... Reality is something infinitely more complex, and the narrow points of view I used all this time seem nothing but silly trivialities."

"I feel so stupid," Kolab thought, "how could I ignore all this time what it means to be trapped in a single point of view? All that arrogance... All this time thinking I knew so much, thinking I was so intelligent, but completely lost in my absurd vanity."

"And it is precisely now, when I have no chance of survival, that I have become aware of it all. Now that it's too late... Even so, thank you, Harun, Aukan, Isabel, Diop... thank you because, even late, I was able to glimpse a truth capable of redeeming all humanity."

"If they could see what I see here inside from out there, if they could feel this multiplicity, they wouldn't be able to avoid changing... they wouldn't be able to avoid overcoming all those egoic thoughts that keep us locked in our petty little battles."

Kolab and Diop continued wandering in complete silence until, at some point, Diop stopped, as if lost in himself.

Kolab looked at Diop as he, in turn, looked at his hands. He no longer knew who he was: Isabel? That name vaguely rang a bell, yet his thick hands didn't seem to fit into all that... Maybe his name was Harun. Yes, that must be it, somehow he remembered that name...

"Diop, listen to me, Diop!"

He looked at her: "Who the hell are you?"

"I'm Kolab, don't you remember me?"

Diop looked at her, confused, unsure of what to think...

"Where...?"

"We're on Pluto, Captain. Remember? Trapped in the labyrinth..."

"My name is... my name is Harun, not Diop... I'm the onboard technician. Yes, that's it, right?"

"Listen to me, You are Captain Diop, those memories aren't yours... It's this place, remember? It tries to confuse us, to mix our memories..."

Diop looked at her, disconnected from reality, without understanding...

"Captain, don't leave me" Kolab said, as desperate tears began to stream down her tense cheeks.

Diop didn't respond, lost in himself, trying to discern which of those identities within him was truly his.

"Who am I?" he muttered.

Kolab, who had until then tried to remain strong and had even believed that Captain Diop was the only one who could keep her safe, became fully aware that even he had lost his battle against this place.

Kolab wept, inconsolably, as she watched Diop showing become less and less conscious. She shook him, even struck him, without getting a reaction. She wandered alone as the dim violet light that bathed the place did the same to her, searching in vain for her own end. However, she found something else...

Suddenly, she found herself in a large stone chamber, in whose center was a small pool of black water, and in the center of it, a shape made of the same liquid seemed to swirl, gradually taking shape and slowly rising above the surface.

The silence was total, absolute. The chamber, lit by that unnatural light that seemed to come from no source, vibrated softly with a frequency more that was felt than heard, as if space itself resonated with its presence.

Kolab held her breath. There was no heat, no cold, no smell. Only stone.

Gradually, the emerging form took on the appearance of Kolab herself, as if it were some kind of three-dimensional mirror. Kolab, wide-eyed, waited in silence, intrigued, her mouth covered by one hand in a gesture of awe.

The details were defined with disturbing precision: the curve of her face, the shine in her eyes, the slight tremble in her lips. It was her... and yet it wasn't. There was something in that liquid, perfect version of herself that made it seem so real...

Finally, the specular Kolab was fully formed, at which moment she spoke with a voice identical t to that of Kolab herself.

"There are places, Kolab, where one cannot go without an invitation, do you understand?"

The voice was like an echo coming from inside her skull. It did not come from the air, but from within her bones.

Kolab remained silent.

"This is not your place..."

Isabel, terrified, still said nothing.

"The universe is a vast place, Kolab... Or should I call you Isabel. Or perhaps Harun. And, of course, it is not what it seems to your eyes."

The entity tilted its head, as if studying her reaction. Its gestures were soft, but they held a latent violence, like a predator enjoying the display of a feigned fragility.

"I understand," Kolab finally managed to say.

"No, Aukan, you understand nothing, you never did and you never will..."

He, being partly Kolab and all the others, swallowed hard.

"Beings like you cannot be allowed to go any further, insects who dare to play with gods without even being aware of the structure of the universe itself. Your father told you that, he punished you, he tried to correct you."

The words struck like whips, but they held no anger. They were simple facts, dictated with the serenity of someone who had pronounced that sentence a thousand times before.

Harun nodded.

"But don't worry, Isabel. You will be a good example for all those who think that going beyond the natural limits established for humanity long ago is a good idea. Isn't it obvious that your place is the planet Earth?"

Chapter 21
The Sea

They recognized themselves as drops of water joining with other drops, forming something greater. Everything made sense and yet, their minds were dissolving, and their souls along with them, as well.

Each drop of water was a mirror reflecting a fragmented, unsustainable reality. It diluted in its own reflection, without origin, without destination, without understanding. They were one. A "one" separated from a whole that, perhaps, could have sustained the leviathan they had become.

The false promises of evolution were no longer even a memory for them, just another wave absorbed by a shore that had completely lost its substance, just as the wave itself had, as well as the water that made it possible.

Diop's forgotten father cradled Kolab in a room unknown to both of them, while Aukan, the ruthless killer, was frightened by the tenderness this father was capable of showing for love of a "daughter" he had never known.

That scene lasted no more than a few seconds, born from a place where time does not exist. Absorbed into itself, it was reborn alongside the savage cry that Isabel let out as she plunged into her truth, which had always been a lie for Harun. Isabel understood it, only to dissolve once again into that sea that was the five crew members of the *Persephone*.

"Is anyone there?"

"Yes, I... I am here," someone without identity answered a question that had already faded away and that he could never hear.

"That narcissus, it's beautiful, isn't it?"

"Go to it, Core, it's for you. I placed it there, just for you..."

"Who are you?" asked the young woman.

"Take the narcissus. Do you think there's any danger in it?"

"No, of course not. How could there be any danger in its beauty?"

And then, when the young woman took the flower in her hands, Hades, Pluto, dragged her into the depths.

"I am Hades, Pluto, the underworld. Here lives death, and here you will live, in my black abode, by my side. Because the stars and the planets do not exist as such. They are only masks of a truth beyond you, Isabel."

"She survived. She became Persephone, goddess of the underworld!"

"She was already a goddess, Isabel... she only needed to be awakened. Her mother refused."

"Yes, my father also wanted to awaken me, now I know. Harun, my son, the world out there is terrible, you must be strong. I do it for your own good, my beloved son. When you grow up, you will understand."

"I never understood. I never listened to you, Father. I know you tried, you did everything you could so that your son would be someone capable of facing the world, and yet... I failed you."

"You did. Your mother and I ended up feeling so much shame… We loved you, Harun, but you failed us. What did we do so wrong, Harun? Wasn't it your fault?"

"Yes, Kolab, it was my fault. Forgive me, you should never have suffered it in your flesh, I should not have let those memories escape me. Don't think it was my father's fault; he loved me. The fault is mine, mine alone, Kolab. Forgive me."

"I'm going to finish you, you damned coward. I've finished off many, and you are only the weakest of them all."

"Do it, Aukan. Obey the Captain, kill me."

"Kill him, it's an order. He's a disgrace to all of us."

He did it; he blew his own brains out, because Harun was no longer something different from Aukan: he was only one more fragment of his own deranged psyche.

"We wanted to be myth. We believed we could overcome difficulties like the heroes and gods of antiquity, but we, the heroes of the Iron Age, crude and mediocre, have perished."

"We are not worthy."

Meanwhile, silence and darkness reigned over the surface of Pluto, above which the Persephone floated silently.

Hybris. That's what they called it in Greece in the days when the last heroes gave way to a decadent age where arrogance took the place of courage and wisdom. Hybris: yes, that was the great sin of those who, in their mediocrity, sought to compare themselves with the gods, believing themselves worthy of apotheosis. Considering themselves equal to Dionysus or Heracles.

Chapter 22
The Awakening

Absolute silence reigned on the bridge of the *Persephone*, in perfect harmony with the outside world. The purple light emerging from the architectural complex on Pluto had completely disappeared, as had the flames of lucidity that once burned within the unfortunate crew of the *Persephone*.

Just as they had arrived, so were the crew members now, occupying their respective seats, their gazes empty and lost in the horizon.

The rescue team that arrived at the scene some time later discovered that none of the crew members had ever left the ship, as had been recorded by the *Persephone* itself. This data left no room for doubt on the matter.

It was also learned that it was the *Persephone's* own A.I. that, seeing their inability to stay alive, provided them with the necessary means to keep them from dying during the time they spent sitting motionless on the bridge.

The Brotherhood transferred them to a secret medical facility not far from Jupiter's moon, Lysithea. It was there that the oracle's message was received with no small amount of dismay by the scientists and members of the clandestine organization. At that point, the dilemma was clear: communicate the message to the appropriate authorities or keep the secret...

The underground conference room was shrouded in gloom. The bluish light from Jovian gas, filtered through the armored glass, created ghostly reflections on the faces of those present. There were nine of them. Only nine. The highest-ranking members of The Brotherhood.

"We cannot ignore this," Dr. Heller said, the xenolinguist. Her voice was dry, almost broken. "This is not a hallucination. All the crew members of the *Persephone* point in the same direction. We've used the most proven techniques of regressive hypnosis on them, and the account we can extract from their broken minds is clear."

"What do you mean?" Brother Rivas asked, newly arrived from Mars.

"I mean that someone or something dwells in those ruins on Pluto. I believe that it is, at the very least, a part of Shub-Niggurath that resides there."

The Elder Brother, almost as old as the cult itself, narrowed his eyes.

"Are you proposing we inform the governments?"

"It's a threat, this could be beyond us. We are putting humanity at risk. Who knows what could happen when another ship finds the place? This was only a warning..."

A murmur ran through the room.

"To warn the governments and provide them with all the necessary materials to support our account could mean the end of our organization," Sister Khalida, High Priestess, intervened.

"You're right, Khalida, but one does not trifle with the gods, and the message is clear: no human must return to that place. At least, not without an invitation..." said Rivas.

Many nodded and showed their agreement with this last statement.

There was a heavy silence. The Elder Brother rose slowly. No one spoke while he stood.

"What happened on Pluto has changed the rules of the game. Eva. The temple. The creatures. And now this. My orders are clear: we must inform the governments. We have time to prepare. It must be done anonymously. Our organization must remain standing. The future is ours."

Printed in Dunstable, United Kingdom